Maxwell Parker, P.I.

Josie Lynn

stepping stones for kids, an imprint of
FOOTEPRINT PRESS
California, USA

Published by Stepping Stones for Kids, an imprint of FootePrint Press.

Publisher's Cataloging-In-Publication Data
(Prepared by The Donohue Group, Inc.)

Lynn, Josie.
   Maxwell Parker, P.I. / Josie Lynn. -- First edition.

      pages ; cm. -- (The Maxwell Parker chronicles ; chapter 1)

   Summary: Twelve-year-old amateur detective Maxwell Parker suspects that her elderly new neighbor has committed murder. With the help of her best friend, Kenneth, Maxwell proceeds to investigate. Meanwhile, having just started junior high, Maxwell must deal with the possibility of losing her best friend to the popular girls, as well as the cost of fitting in.
   Interest age level: 011-013.
   Issued also as an ebook.
   ISBN: 978-0-9904353-2-7

   1. Teenage girls--Juvenile fiction. 2. Best friends--Juvenile fiction. 3. Murder--Investigation--Juvenile fiction. 4. Neighbors--Juvenile fiction. 5. Teenage girls--Fiction. 6. Best friends--Fiction. 7. Murder--Fiction. 8. Neighbors--Fiction. 9. Mystery and detective stories. 10. Mystery fiction. I. Title.

PZ7.L966 Ma 2014
[Fic]   2014941472

for my loving family

contents

1. Mrs. Cook

Riverdale was in the middle of a heat wave and Maxwell Parker was parched. The heat, she liked to imagine, was the result of a large, bad-mannered, fire-breathing dragon flying overhead who would not be content until he singed every last hair on the head of every last Riverdale resident. Whether or not this was the true cause of the heat, it had the additional and undesired effect of turning everyone's lawn a decided warm, dry yellow.

Maxwell sat on her front porch, scanning Mulberry Avenue. The heat rising from the asphalt made everything appear to shimmer and ripple, as if she was watching the world from the dry side of a wet windowpane.

She was trying to decide whether she should skate up the street or not. She had gone to the trouble of putting on her in-line skates, but the dragon-breathed heat was rapidly zapping her strength.

Maxwell fanned her face with a limp hand but only succeeded in directing more hot air her way.

I might as well be in Afghanistan, she thought.

A Jeep careened down Mulberry Avenue and came to a screeching halt in front of the Millers' house across the street.

Oh, no, Maxwell thought, *rebel troops.* Her heart did a flip-flop. Her breathing quickened. She had to be ready to spring on a moment's notice.

She blinked several times. Through the heat, she thought she could make out a group of armed soldiers jumping out of the Jeep and running towards the Millers' house. The front door opened and the group went inside.

A safe house! Maxwell thought.

Soon the street would be lined with concertina wire, making escape impossible.

Good thing she was wearing skates after all. Now the trick would be locating a breach in the perimeter.

Maxwell turned at the sound of animated conversation coming from the Millers' house. The door opened again and the group, now accompanied by the Millers' teenage son, piled into the Jeep and drove off.

Maxwell heard pop music blasting from the stereo. Peals of laughter wafted out from the open car. The mirage dissipated, and Maxwell's clear vision was restored.

Just a bunch of teenagers going to the mall, she thought, disgusted.

Nothing exciting ever happened in Riverdale.

Maxwell sighed. The truth was she was bored.

She had spent the entire summer hoping for something, anything, even remotely interesting to happen. Now summer vacation was almost over and nothing but dull monotony loomed ahead: a new school year, new homework, and new teachers, but otherwise the same old same old.

The only nearly interesting thing that happened all summer was that someone finally bought the house directly across the street from the Parkers' house. All summer Maxwell watched as potential buyers came to look at the house. Some seemed promising. Most, however, seemed dreadfully ordinary. The person who ultimately bought the house was an elderly woman who called herself Mrs. Cook.

Maxwell and her mom met her yesterday. Mrs. Cook had come over to ask Mrs. Parker if she could borrow a tape measure. Mrs. Parker sent Maxwell to search for it, but Maxwell heard enough of the conversation—full of "how are you's?" and "fine, thanks, and you's?" and "my, isn't it hot's?"—to know that Mrs. Cook was just another unremarkable Riverdale resident: nice, polite, proper, and boring.

Why couldn't a nice mob family or a gang of robbers move into the neighborhood? At least they'd do something.

Now Maxwell was angry that she volunteered to take Mrs. Cook some of the gingersnaps her mother made the night before.

Maxwell sighed again.

Under normal circumstances, she would go next door and bug her best friend, Kenneth. However, Kenneth had been away at basketball camp all summer and had just returned yesterday. To go running to him the second he got back would be tantamount to telling him she missed him.

Maxwell bit her lip. She just couldn't go over there. She just couldn't tell Kenneth how, without him, she'd felt like a balloon that someone had forgotten to knot, puttering around briefly before unceremoniously landing in a lifeless heap on the front lawn.

She was wearing cut-off denim shorts and a yellow tee shirt that had belonged to her mother when she had been a teenager. The shirt had brown lettering that read: *Spoiled & Lovin' It.* Maxwell found it in a pile of clothes that her mom was donating to Goodwill.

"Why are you getting rid of this?" she had asked holding the shirt up.

"It's a dumb sentiment," her mom had answered, but Maxwell remembered seeing an old snapshot of her mom wearing the shirt, standing in front of a gas station, squinting and smiling at the camera.

"An ill-advised road trip," was how her mom had described it, laughing. "Your dad's idea."

Her mom looked so young and happy in the photograph, so present and in the moment, as if the camera had magically been able to transform her into some other person. Maxwell hardly remembered seeing her mom look so carefree. More often than not, these days, her brows were knitted into a look of intense concentration and her mind seemed to be light years away.

Maxwell liked wearing the vintage tee shirt. Even though it in no way, shape, or form described her current situation, she thought the sentiment was full of possibilities.

The minutes ticked by. Maxwell looked at her watch. It was 10:53.

Just then, she heard the door open next door and Kenneth Newman said, "Okay, Mom, I'll water the flowers."

Maxwell almost stopped breathing. Kenneth was coming out.

She heard his footsteps on the driveway and a faint "thump, thump," so she knew he had his basketball with him. Sometimes she thought he must have somehow had it surgically implanted to his hand.

Whatever, she thought. *If I was going to develop a hobby, you can bet it would be something useful, like knitting or glass blowing.*

Kenneth turned the hose on and started to water his mother's geraniums.

He'd come back from basketball camp taller and even cuter.

He turned his head toward Maxwell's house, but he didn't see her because the giant Indian rubber tree was between them.

How did that song go? Something about an ant and a rubber tree?

Focus, Maxwell, focus.

She didn't exactly want to see Kenneth just yet, so she sneaked inside, sight unseen.

Stopping briefly at the door to remove her in-line skates, Maxwell took a moment to assess the situation. She knew her mother was in the den because that was where the smell of paint was coming from. Plus, as she sneaked past the den, she could hear her mother's faint humming. That could only mean one thing: her mother was in "the zone."

Maxwell went upstairs to her bedroom.

She went to her window and looked out over Mulberry Avenue. Kenneth was still in front of his house. Maxwell picked up her binoculars and trained them on Kenneth.

As if he sensed her presence, he looked up at her window. Seeing her, he smiled and waved.

Maxwell almost dropped her binoculars.

"Whatcha doing?" Kenneth mouthed.

"Nothing much," Maxwell mouthed back.

"Come down," Kenneth said, nodding and smiling.

Maxwell nodded back and pointed to her watch, to indicate she'd be down in a minute. She checked the time. A good ten minutes had passed since the last time she checked. This might be a good time to ask her mom about the cookies, but first, she would try to locate them herself.

Maxwell gingerly placed her binoculars on her desk and went to the kitchen.

Stacks of dirty dishes were piled up in the sink and on the counter. Mrs. Parker's laptop was sitting open on the breakfast bar. The box of cereal from this morning's breakfast was still on the counter.

Maxwell looked in several cabinets but found no cookies.

She burst into the den where her mother sat at her worktable, painting a tiny ceramic house.

Zero reaction, not even a glance in her direction.

Maxwell sighed. She knew her mother was an artist and that painting tiny, detailed houses required intense concentration, but this was ridiculous.

"Mom!" she said quite loudly. When there was no response, she added, "What did you do with the cookies?"

Mrs. Parker continued to paint.

Maxwell gave an exasperated exclamation and stomped out of the room.

"Honey," her mother called absently after her, "were you talking to me?"

Maxwell knew her mother loved her, but she sometimes wondered if she could see her. She stuck her head back in the den and asked in an icy tone: "Cookies? For Mrs. Cook?"

"They're in the dishwasher, honey," her mother answered. "There were too many dirty dishes on the counter."

"Oh, of course," Maxwell said. She hoped her mother would catch the sarcasm dripping from her voice. "That makes perfect sense. Why didn't I think of that?"

No response, just faint humming.

"Well, I hope they're not wet," Maxwell said, opening the dishwasher and pulling out a plastic wrapped plate piled high with gingersnaps.

"Why would they be wet?" her mother called. "The dishwasher's broken. Remind me to call a repair man, will you?"

Maxwell put the cookies on the table near the front door, then went upstairs to get a pair of shoes. Every shoe she owned was under her bed, but Maxwell couldn't find two that matched, except for a pair of hiking boots with red laces.

She grabbed a navy-blue pinstriped vest she had discovered while rummaging through her brother's closet. The vest was too large for her, but it was just the thing a P.I. would wear in one of those black and white detective movies she liked to watch on AMC. Besides, it helped Maxwell think. She put it on over her vintage tee.

She was about to run back downstairs when she noticed her fishing hat lying on the floor beside her bed. She dusted it off and put it on.

"You're not wearing that, are you?" her mother asked as Maxwell passed her on the way to the door.

Maxwell looked down at her clothes. "Something wrong with my outfit?"

"It's rather unusual, don't you think? You'll startle Mrs. Cook. She's such a sweet, old-fashioned lady. Maybe a nice dress would be better."

"It's too hot for anything besides shorts," Maxwell said, opening the front door.

"Maybe if you took off the hat," Mrs. Parker suggested.

"You can't be serious," Maxwell protested, "this is my deducing hat. I have to wear it."

"Maxwell, you're not thinking of pulling any funny business, are you?"

"Me? Funny business? Mom, when have I ever—?"

"Plenty of times. Now give me a kiss and you behave yourself."

"I know how to behave," Maxwell said, blowing her mother a kiss.

"Yes, but the question is, will you?" Mrs. Parker laughed.

Ha, ha, Maxwell thought.

She made a mental note that if she ever had children she wouldn't make lame jokes when they were trying to be dignified and grown up.

Carefully balancing the plate of cookies in one hand, Maxwell grabbed her tan leather knapsack, which she slung across her chest so no one would be able to snatch it from her. She gave her deducing hat a final tug and stepped outside where Kenneth was waiting for her.

"Hey, Max, where're you going?" he called, walking towards the Parkers' house.

Maxwell tried to suppress a smile. "Do you want something in particular?" she asked sternly, just in case he might have thought she was glad to see him.

"Not really."

"Well, I'm extremely busy." Maxwell pushed past him and started across the street.

"Come on, Max. What are you up to?"

Maxwell stopped in the middle of the street. "That is none of your business, Kenneth Newman." She made her voice dignified. Holding her plate of cookies, she marched to Mrs. Cook's front door and rang the doorbell.

From Mrs. Cook's open kitchen window came a wonderful smell that Maxwell immediately recognized as freshly baked brownies.

"Yes, yes," she heard Mrs. Cook say through the open window. She was apparently on the phone. "But it isn't simply a matter of right and wrong, the question is, can I get away with it?" Mrs. Cook laughed. "That's going to be the trick. Getting away with it."

That's odd, Maxwell thought. *Getting away with what?*

She rang the bell again.

"Yes, Dear, but I have to go," Mrs. Cook said. "Someone's at the door. We'll finish this later."

Maxwell heard Mrs. Cook hang the phone up. Then she heard footsteps approaching the door and the door opened.

"Well, hello there, Maxwell," Mrs. Cook said cheerfully. "Come on in."

If Maxwell had been casting a movie for an old-fashioned grandmother, Mrs. Cook would have gotten the role, hands down. She was smallish and slightly plump and spoke with a sweet voice that sounded as if she was always smiling. She seemed to always wear a ruffled apron with a floral print. She smelled warm and sugary, like baked goods. However, what took the proverbial cake, in Maxwell's opinion, was Mrs. Cook's hair. Every time Maxwell had seen her, it had been skillfully arranged into what looked exactly like a perfect silvery-blue beehive. Maxwell imagined Mrs. Cook must sit for hours in a hair salon and use tons of hairspray to get it to look like that. In a way, she looked like Marge Simpson.

"Come on in, dear. Make yourself at home," Mrs. Cook said, leading her into the living room. "Can I get you some brownies?"

"No, thank you," Maxwell said. She didn't want to eat anything from Mrs. Cook. Her Rule Number One of Food Safety was, do not take food from highly suspicious people. Mrs. Cook's comments on the telephone had elevated her from the nice, polite, proper and boring category to the irregular and highly suspicious category.

"Well, how about something cool to drink? It's hot."

"I'll take a 7-up, in a can, if you have any." Maxwell hoped she was following her mother's orders to behave. She placed the cookies on the end table next to her chair.

When Mrs. Cook brought the can, Maxwell inspected it carefully. Nothing was leaking from it, so she figured it must be safe. Cans, she decided, were definitely safer than glasses. You could always tell if someone tried to lace a can with a foreign substance, but someone could easily slip a mickey into a drink served in a glass without detection.

After meticulously wiping the rim of her can with a napkin, she opened it and took a sip.

Maxwell knew better than to take people at face value. People never came right out and said they were trying to poison you. First they acted nice and charming, to lure you in. The next thing you knew, you were clutching your throat and gasping for air as they watched with a maniacal grin, rubbing their hands in glee.

Maxwell surveyed the room carefully. The sofa and over-stuffed armchairs were all upholstered in the same chintzy-looking flowery fabric. The coffee table looked like an old chest and was draped with a shawl woven with rich, exotic colors. The built-in bookcases that lined the walls were filled with books.

Evil Under the Sun, A Murder is Announced, Murder on the Orient Express, Death on the Nile, Maxwell silently read off a few titles. They all sounded so bloody and completely out of place in so bright and cheery a room.

There's definitely something amiss here, Maxwell thought, but she couldn't put her finger on what it was.

"You must like mysteries," she said aloud, while she tried to think. "Murder mysteries."

"Yes," Mrs. Cook agreed, "especially Agatha Christie."

On closer inspection, all of the books did seem to be Agatha Christie. Miss Marple. Inspector Hercule Poirot. Sometimes they played his movies on TV, and Maxwell loved the funny little man with the handlebar moustache.

"Do you like any other authors?" Maxwell asked.

"Well, you might say Agatha Christie is my idol. I get a lot of inspiration from her books. My husband and I used to read her together, just before going to bed."

Murder seems like a strange topic to read about at bedtime, Maxwell thought. "I didn't realize you were married," she said aloud.

"Well, I was. My husband's dead," Mrs. Cook said in her cheerful voice.

"I'm sorry," Maxwell said, but mentally she noted that down as yet another odd thing that didn't fit.

"He's been gone for some time now, but I still miss him, of course," Mrs. Cook said quietly.

Maxwell sensed that the prolonged discussion about the late Mr. Cook was making Mrs. Cook sad. Of course, Maxwell realized it could all be an act. Murderers in movies were always very good at pretending to be surprised and sad. Nevertheless, she decided it was best to drop the subject.

"That was his favorite chair," Mrs. Cook said, nodding towards Maxwell.

"I'm sorry. I didn't know." Maxwell started to stand up. "I can sit someplace else."

Mrs. Cook grasped Maxwell's arm. Tightly. "You'll do no such thing," she said.

Maxwell's arm throbbed with pain. Mrs. Cook had incredible strength and surprisingly quick reflexes for a woman her age.

"I brought you some cookies," Maxwell said to change the subject. She tried to smile as she rubbed her arm. "My mother baked them, but it was my idea. Just a little house-warming present." She handed the cookies to Mrs. Cook.

"How sweet of you!" Mrs. Cook took the plate and placed it on the coffee table.

Maxwell stared at the coffee table in shock. Suddenly she knew her suspicions about Mrs. Cook weren't far-fetched at all.

She was in the living room of a murderer!

2. The Coffee Table

If Mrs. Cook had taken the cookies into the kitchen, maybe her crime would have gone undetected. Perhaps Maxwell would have gone home, never giving that coffee table a second thought, and she would have continued to think of Mrs. Cook as a sweet, harmless grandmother whose main concern was getting away with crossing the street on a "don't walk" signal or not flossing every day.

However, by placing the cookies on the coffee table, Mrs. Cook forced Maxwell to take a long hard look at it, and this set in motion a chain reaction that caused her brain to start churning out possibilities. Once she reached the possibility of the matter, the probability was a leap so inconsequential it was barely worth noting.

Now Maxwell understood what was amiss. Now she knew exactly what Mrs. Cook meant when she said the trick would be getting away with it. Mrs. Cook was talking about getting away with murder!

Maxwell had seen something like this on Turner Classic Movies—an old Alfred Hitchcock movie about a guy who murdered his friend and hid him in a wooden chest, which he covered with a piece of cloth because he didn't have time to dispose of the body properly before his dinner guests arrived.

On close inspection, Maxwell realized that Mrs. Cook's coffee table looked just like that chest and that it was large enough to hold a human body.

Maxwell shuddered. That was all it would be after it was dead—a body, a corpse, not even a person anymore. The thought was gruesome, but after all, she told herself, murder is gruesome.

"Would you like to see my family album?" Mrs. Cook asked, jarring Maxwell out of her thoughts.

Mrs. Cook pulled an ancient-looking photo album from one of the many bookcases in her living room and began to show Maxwell her childhood pictures. Maxwell usually enjoyed looking at pictures, especially pictures of people when they were younger. She almost felt sorry that Mrs. Cook was a murderer. They could have been good friends otherwise.

"Should I leave my can in the kitchen?" Maxwell asked when it was time to go home.

"No, just give it to me, Maxwell. I haven't unpacked the kitchen yet. It still looks like a tornado hit."

I'll just bet, Maxwell thought. *I wonder what she's really trying to hide. More dead bodies?*

Mrs. Cook returned from the kitchen and, as she walked Maxwell to the door, Maxwell happened to glance at her blouse. Right below her chest was a dark stain. The stain was deep reddish-brown in color, like dried blood. Maxwell hadn't noticed it before, because Mrs. Cook's apron had been hiding it.

She quickly thanked Mrs. Cook and rushed out of the house.

Once outside, she leaned against Mrs. Cook's garage to catch her breath.

"It's worse than I thought," she said to the cat lounging on the driveway. When he didn't answer, she added, "All right, it might have been chocolate from the brownies."

Then it occurred to her that may be what Mrs. Cook wanted her to think. Perhaps she only made the brownies so that any bloodstains around the house would be mistaken for chocolate.

Mrs. Cook—if that was indeed her name—was very smart, but not smarter than the world famous detective, Maxwell Parker.

Okay, so I'm not exactly world famous, yet, Maxwell had to admit. *But I will be when I bring that murderous widow to justice. I'll have this case wrapped up before the police even know there is a case. That ought to be enough to turn my life story into a movie.*

Maxwell could see it now. *A Mind for Crime: The Maxwell Parker Story.* It would air on Lifetime or the Hallmark Channel or OWN. She'd be so famous that other famous people would be clamoring to meet her. She could see the opening now...

"Maxwell, over here!" the paparazzi would call.

"Who are you wearing?"

"This old thing?" she'd demur...

"Max! Max! Ma-ax!"

Maxwell looked up. Kenneth was standing on the sidewalk across the street, dribbling a basketball and screaming at her.

Maxwell crossed the street.

"Kenneth, were you watching when Mrs. Cook moved in yesterday?"

"It just so happens, I was. I had just gotten home."

"Did you notice anything peculiar?"

"Peculiar in what way?"

"Anything odd. Anything that didn't seem to fit."

"Well, she has a very large refrigerator. They had to remove the front door to get the fridge in."

"Anything else?"

"Tell me what you were doing over there, first."

"You are infuriating, Kenneth Newman, I swear." Maxwell looked at Kenneth, who looked right back at her.

"Oh, all right," Maxwell said finally. "We were talking. Is that all right with you? Now, if you don't have any information for me, I have to go. I'm pretty busy."

Kenneth looked hurt. "I'm bored, Max. I thought maybe we could do something together." He had stopped dribbling his basketball.

Maxwell attempted to look annoyed, even though she was pleased to know Kenneth still considered her his friend.

"Was there anyone with Mrs. Cook yesterday?"

"Well, there was that man."

"What man? Why didn't you mention him before?"

"You asked if there was anything peculiar. He wasn't peculiar, he was just a man."

"Was he a friend of hers? I mean, are you sure he wasn't one of the movers?"

"Yes. He was older. About Mrs. Cook's age."

"Well, what happened to him? Did he leave?"

"I didn't see him leave. I'd probably already gone inside by then."

"Or maybe he didn't leave. At least, not out of the front door."

"What are you talking about, Max?"

"I have a theory."

"About the old man at Mrs. Cook's house?" Kenneth asked. "What kind of theory? What's this all about, Max? You're not thinking about investigating Mrs. Cook, are you?"

"What if I am?"

"Well, before you do any funny stuff, I think you should just Google her."

"Google her?" Maxwell scoffed. "You can't believe everything you read on the Internet, Kenny. How gullible are you?"

"I'm not. I just think it would save you from wasting valuable time investigating some totally innocent person, while hardened criminals go free. Come on, Max, she's just a little old lady."

"And the swine flu is just an inconvenience. Besides, she may be old, but she's strong. And she's weird."

"Since when is being weird against the law? If it was, they'd have put you in jail a long time ago."

"What's that suppose to mean?" Maxwell demanded.

"Well, your clothes, and that backpack you always carry, even when we're not in school—"

"Look, my clothes are my business, okay? This is a knapsack, not a backpack as you very ignorantly put it. My knapsack is very special to me—it belonged to my father and traveled all around the world with him when he was a foreign correspondent. It's practically the only thing I have left of his.

If you think I'm so embarrassing to be around, you can just go home."

"That's not what I meant, Max. I was just trying to make a point. You have a unique way of dressing. No one else in school dresses like you. Some people might think you're a little strange. Like my sister and her friends. But I told them you're not. See, they don't know you. They're judging you from your appearance. People shouldn't do that." He looked at Maxwell. Her head was down. She was kicking a clump of grass growing between a crack in the sidewalk with the toe of her hiking boot.

"Sabrina thinks I'm weird?"

"Well, yes, Max. A lot of the girls do. I'm sorry, I shouldn't have said anything."

"And you defended me?"

"Well, I had to say something. They were talking about my bud. Besides, I think you look kind of cute." There was an uncomfortable silence. "Here, have a candy bar," Kenneth said. He took a candy bar out of his pocket and held it out for Maxwell to divide.

"Thanks, Kenny." Maxwell split the candy bar in two. She gave the unwrapped half to Kenneth and put the other half in her knapsack.

Kenneth shoved the candy bar into his mouth. "Well," he said with his mouth full, "the important thing is that we're still friends. I'll see you tomorrow."

Kenneth picked up his basketball and went into his house through the open garage.

Maxwell went inside, too, but not before making a mental note to be nicer to Kenneth in the future, even if he was acting his age.

3. Dexter and Spot

"What were you and Kenneth talking about out there?" A familiar voice greeted Maxwell when she opened the front door.

"Dexter! I didn't know you were home!" Maxwell ran to her brother.

He picked her up and swung her around. "Spot, you haven't grown at all."

"Well, I'm trying but I have zero control over growth spurts. I see you're developing nicely, though." Maxwell put both of her hands around Dexter's forearm.

"Yeah, well, I've been working out a little," Dexter said modestly. "Coach says it will improve my game."

"No doubt Angelica will agree," Maxwell said.

"Spot, where do you get these scandalous things you say? I'm telling mom to cancel cable. In the meantime, what am I going to do with you?" Dexter grabbed Maxwell, turned her upside down, and carried her into the kitchen.

Maxwell screamed with laughter.

"Dexter, if you don't put me down, I'll—"

"Do what? Yell? No one will hear you. Mom's at the art supply store."

"I don't care, put me down!" The blood rushing to Maxwell's head made her dizzy. Her deducing hat had fallen off.

Dexter deposited her on the kitchen counter.

"So, what was that comment about my girlfriend?" he wanted to know.

"I wasn't trying to be scandalous, if that's what you thought. I'm just saying she looks at you like a piece of meat, and I think there's a lot more to you than that."

Dexter was quiet for a minute. Maxwell hoped he wouldn't be mad at her, but finally he said, "You know, you could be right. Maybe she doesn't appreciate the whole me. What do you propose I do?"

"I think Angelica's a little shallow. You should help her develop depth. If that doesn't work, maybe you'll have to dump her."

"It's so simple when you say it, Spot, but did you ever stop to think that I might be in love?"

With her? The thought was so ludicrous that Maxwell almost laughed, but she only smiled wisely and said, "Love is very complicated, isn't it?"

Dexter tugged Maxwell's hair. "You're cute." He went to the refrigerator and started rummaging through it. "Where's the Coke?"

"We don't have Coke. Only ginger ale and 7-up. Unless you want something in a red can called 'cola.' It's not very good, but we have lots of it. Mom went crazy at the Grocery Club again."

"How about two ginger ales, then?"

"That sounds good," Maxwell said.

Dexter brought two cans of ginger ale to the counter where Maxwell was sitting and handed one to her.

"I don't drink cola anymore," she told him. "Too much caffeine. I'm trying to limit my caffeine intake."

"I see," Dexter said. If Maxwell didn't know better, she would have thought he wanted to laugh.

"And I'm trying to cut back on this. Do you know how much sugar is in one twelve ounce soft drink can?"

Dexter shook his head.

"Ten teaspoons. I read it on the Internet. You might as well eat a bowl of sugar. The only hard part is I happen to like soft drinks, except, of course, cola."

"Well, Spot, I'm sure you'll work it out."

Maxwell nodded. "So, Dexter, have you been able to switch your major, yet?"

"That's a little complicated," Dexter said.

"Why? Have you talked to Mom?"

"That's what makes it complicated."

"Dex, I really don't think she'll care. She just wants us to be happy. Isn't that what she always says? All of that stuff about 'finding your bliss.'"

"It's just that I've wanted to be a journalist since I was six years old. I think Mom had her heart set on me following in Dad's footsteps, Spot."

"Oh. I hadn't thought about it like that."

Dexter tousled Maxwell's hair. "Well, that's all I keep thinking about. I just don't want to disappoint her."

"But, if you want to be a psychologist—" Maxwell began, smoothing her hair down.

"That's just it," Dexter interrupted. "Do I?" He rubbed his temples and groaned. "I took some psych classes, Spot, and I liked them. But does that mean I'd be a good psychologist? I mean, I know I'd be a good journalist. I was the editor of the high school newspaper for three years straight. What if I'm lousy at helping people?" Dexter put his head on the counter.

Maxwell looked shocked. She couldn't fathom the idea that Dexter could be lousy at anything. She stroked his hair soothingly.

After a while, Dexter lifted his head up. "Well, enough about me," he said. "Let's talk about you."

Maxwell studied Dexter's face. The stress lines were starting to fade. He was almost smiling. "Well, okay. I suppose I can tell you what I've decided. I've decided what I want to be when I grow up."

"Oh, it's so easy for you, is it?" Dexter said. Now he was really smiling. "What's that, Spot?"

"A gumshoe, a P.I., a private detective."

"I thought you wanted to be a female Harry Connick, Jr."

Maxwell took a long sip of ginger ale.

Summertime at the Hollywood Bowl…

The sun was setting and the stars were just starting to rise. The air was crisp and cool, as if the day had just emerged from a refreshing shower. Maxwell walked onto the stage and stared out, past the floodlights, into the audience.

She felt the energy from the crowd embrace and lift her.

"Good evening, Hollywood!" she called into the microphone. "Are you ready for some noise?"

The orchestra began the opening bars of her latest hit and, as Maxwell sat down at the piano, the crowd began to scream and cheer. In the wings, her biggest fan, Kenneth, was grinning like crazy and giving her thumbs up…

"Well, maybe," she told Dexter. "But it would depend. Maybe I could do both. Investigating by day, music by night."

"Of course," Dexter said, smiling, "my bad."

"Anyway, the important news is, I have a case." She looked at Dexter to see his reaction.

His eyes widened satisfactorily. "Really? Someone hired you?"

"No, it's, uh, something I stumbled on. See, there's this old lady, and she..."

Before Maxwell could continue, the phone rang. She grabbed the receiver from its nearby cradle.

"Hello.... Yes, this is Maxwell. Hello, Angelica." Maxwell sighed and glanced at Dexter. He looked eager and expectant. *He's in love,* she thought sadly.

"Yes, Dexter just so happens to be here. We were just talking." Maxwell was about to add "about you" but decided against it. "Yes, I'll get him for you. Nice talking to you Angelica," she said sweetly.

Maxwell gave the phone to Dexter, and as she left the kitchen, she heard him saying, "Hello, Honey, I missed you."

She went to her room and debated whether she should cry or not. She wanted to. Dexter had been going to school and working in the Bay Area all summer. This was probably his only visit home, and here he was wasting their precious time together talking to Angelica on the phone.

Plain and simple, Maxwell adored her big brother. He was more like a father to her, since their father died when she was four years old. Dexter was the only person in the whole world who called her Spot.

She had heard the story of how it began many times. Dexter wanted a dog, but their parents wouldn't get one for him, so news of a new baby sister made him furious. "I asked for a puppy and you got *that*?" he'd said the first time he saw her. In his distain, he christened her "Spot."

Maxwell hated to hear her brother call Angelica "Honey." Honey was something you call someone you cared a great deal about, like your child, or your wife! At least he didn't call her Spot.

There was a knock on her door. Dexter opened it and peeked in.

"Spot, I'm picking Angelica up. We're going out for Thai. Want to come?"

"No, I'll find something here. Mom will be back soon, I hope."

"Well, if you're sure," Dexter said, hugging her, "I'll see you later."

"Should I wait up?"

"Yes, I'll be home early," Dexter said and left.

Maxwell dropped her deducing hat on the floor. She opened her knapsack and began emptying it onto her bed. A notebook, a pair of sunglasses, a change of clothes, a dictionary, a report on the rain forest from sixth grade, and finally, an MP3 player.

Maxwell found Alanis Morissette's *Ironic* on her MP3 player, because it seemed appropriate to her mood. As she listened to the music, she spied on Mrs. Cook through her binoculars. Mrs. Cook was digging at the side of her house.

Aha, thought Maxwell. She wrote this down in her notebook:

The Maxwell Parker Files.

Case No. 0362—The Cook Murders.

Fact #1: Mrs. Cook is trying to "get away" with something.

Fact #2: Mrs. Cook has a coffee table that is large enough to hold a corpse.

Fact #3: There was a bloodstain on her shirt.

Fact #4: Kenneth saw a man at Mrs. Cook's house on moving day. His whereabouts are currently unaccounted for.

Fact #5: At 6:09 this evening, I saw the suspect digging a large hole in her backyard.

Fact #6: Mrs. Cook describes her husband as dead, but does not seem very sad about it.

Possibility #1: Maybe Mrs. Cook murdered her husband.

Possibility #2: Maybe the man Kenneth saw was, in reality, Mrs. Cook's husband.

Probability #1: Mrs. Cook killed this man and is hiding him in her coffee table.

Probability #2: Mrs. Cook intends to bury her victim/husband in her backyard.

She closed her notebook, turned her MP3 player off, and went downstairs to find something to eat.

She was warming up some leftover lasagna in the microwave when her mother came in.

"How was your day, sweetheart?" Mrs. Parker said, giving her a peck on the cheek. "Did Mrs. Cook like the cookies?"

"Mom, sit down. Have some lasagna. I'll tell you all about my day." Maxwell handed a plate to her mother. She took another plate to her seat.

"Mrs. Cook seemed to appreciate the cookies. She told me to thank you. But, Mother, I have something to tell you that might disturb you."

Mrs. Parker raised her eyebrows expectantly.

"Mom, I think Mrs. Cook killed her husband."

Mrs. Parker dropped her fork. "Oh, Maxwell, not again. Honey, we've been through this before, your imagination has gotten out of control again."

"I'm not imagining things, Mom. I don't do that."

Mrs. Parker raised her eyebrows again.

"I admit the time I thought Anderson Cooper worked at Riverdale Cinema was going a little overboard, but—"

"A little? Maxwell, you and Kenneth followed the poor man home, insisting you knew who he was, and demanding that he tell you what it was really like to 'keep them honest,'" her mother said making air quotes with her fingers.

"Mother, we didn't demand anything. We simply suggested that he give up his charade since we had figured out who he really was. But that was a long time ago. I've matured a lot since then."

"That was last year. Anyway, I hope you've learned your lesson. You can't go around harassing innocent people just because you have a hunch," Mrs. Parker said.

"Yeah, well, I thought CNN had sent him in response to my letter about the Riverdale Water and Power cover-up."

"Maxwell, there was no cover-up," Mrs. Parker said.

"The water was brown for three whole days, and they repeatedly ignored my calls about it. If it had been something serious they should have, at least, alerted the public. People die from drinking contaminated water."

"Fortunately, no one died."

"How do you know? They could have covered that up, too. That's why I wanted Anderson Cooper to come investigate."

"And as you can see, CNN didn't deem it necessary. Instead, they sent his look-alike, poor man," Mrs. Parker said, laughing.

"Well, he was very nice about it. He gave us his autograph. I still have it, too. 'To Maxwell Parker, Best Wishes, Love, Willie Jones.' And he did look like Anderson Cooper, except he was shorter, and probably a little older. I mean, his hair was really white, not prematurely white, like Anderson's. Anyway, if you had seen him, you'd have thought he was Anderson Cooper, too."

"But I wouldn't have followed him home."

"And if it had been him, you would have missed out. Sometimes, despite how unlikely something may seem, you have to take a chance. Take Mrs. Cook—"

"Let's not."

"But, Mom, all of the signs are there. Her behavior is very suspicious. She has a collection of Agatha Christie murder mysteries. She says they 'inspire' her. What's that supposed to mean? And Kenneth said he saw a man over there the day she moved in—where is he now? Then she wouldn't let me into the kitchen, because it was dirty. Come on, she just moved in. How dirty could it be? And," she looked at her mother to emphasize the importance of this next statement, "there was blood on her shirt."

"Blood, Maxwell?"

"Yes, Mother, blood. Okay, it could have been the chocolate from the brownies, but it really looked more like blood. I'm sure it was blood, especially now, since I saw her digging in the backyard."

"Digging in her backyard? Have you ever heard of gardening? I do it all the time, and I can't be certain, but I believe even you have been known to garden, on occasion. Leave the poor woman alone, all right? Promise me that, Sweetie." Mrs. Parker looked amused and this infuriated Maxwell.

"Well, I was just warning you, Mother. She might be a dangerous psychopath, for all we know."

"Then maybe the course of wisdom would be for you to stay away from her, too."

"It's not fair," Maxwell muttered.

"Excuse me, Honey, did you grumble something?" Mrs. Parker asked. "I'm sorry, I didn't quite catch it."

"I said, 'It's not fair.' It's not fair that people like Nancy Drew and Veronica Mars are always stumbling across full-fledged mysteries that they get to solve and nothing even remotely interesting ever happens to me."

"First of all, Maxwell, Nancy Drew and Veronica Whoever are fictional characters. Those stories are all dreamed up in someone's head. It's not real life. Secondly, in real life, mysteries are messy. People get hurt. Corpses bleed. It's not interesting or exciting. It's scary, not to mention dangerous."

"Well, if you'll excuse me, *Criminal Minds* is coming on."

"Don't let me keep you from that," Mrs. Parker said. "Since you made dinner, I'll do the dishes."

Maxwell went into the den and turned on the TV. A re-run of *Criminal Minds* was just starting. Maxwell loved the BAU team, especially Dr. Reid. He was so smart, and hardly ever used a weapon, other than his brilliant mind.

4. Late Night Spying

Maxwell was washing dishes when Dexter came home.

"How was your hot date?" she asked.

"It was great. We went to the art gallery and then we saw a foreign film. I tried to take your advice about helping her develop depth."

"What's the prognosis?"

"Well, it's a start. Although she did say she didn't like the movie because she doesn't like to read."

"I'm glad you had a nice time." Maxwell tried to like Angelica, but all Angelica ever talked about was makeup and clothes. Maxwell was disappointed that Dexter was attracted to someone so superficial. She wished he would date someone she had more in common with, or at least someone he had more in common with.

Once she overheard Angelica tell Dexter, "Maxwell's a pretty girl, but she doesn't do anything with her looks. Do you think she would mind if I gave her some makeup tips?"

The ultimate nerve. Maxwell wasn't interested in Angelica's beauty tips. In fact, she didn't think much about beauty at all, except to hope that she would grow up to be very beautiful, the way most of her favorite heroines always seemed to.

For now, she was content with her shoulder-length black hair, large, long-lashed brown eyes, big, friendly smile, and a dimple in each of her cheeks. Maxwell considered the dimples a curse because she couldn't think of one famous detective who had dimples. They all had their quirks but never dimples.

"How was your evening?" Dexter asked.

"Boring, as usual."

"Is that right? Does it get pretty dull around here, Spot?"

"Well," Maxwell said, "it's a lot quieter when you're away."

"School will be starting soon. That'll give you something to do."

"Dexter, I have something I want to ask you."

"Shoot." Dexter leaned against the counter.

"Okay. So, how do you recognize a murderer?"

"They have little beady eyes," he said, laughing.

"Come on, Dex, I'm serious. How can you tell if someone's capable of murder?"

Dexter thought for a minute. "Spot, I can't tell you how a murderer looks because, the truth is, being a murderer doesn't make you look any different from anyone else. In fact, anyone can be a murderer. Kenneth, you, me, the old lady across the street. Anyone."

"Well, then, can you tell by their disposition?"

"Not necessarily. People can disguise the way they are inside. Besides, some psychopaths act perfectly normal—then they change—like Jekyll and Hyde."

Maxwell stopped washing the dishes. "Yes," she said, "I've read about that. And maybe a slight slip-up betrays them. So, what you're saying is that anyone can be a murderer, even the most innocent-looking person."

"Well, you can't be paranoid, but it is possible."

"And all of those people on the news who get arrested for murder—they have to be someone's neighbor, right?"

"Sure. And don't their neighbors always say, 'He was such a nice man, who would have ever thought he'd do something like that?'"

Maxwell pulled the stopper out of the sink and watched the water drain as Dexter's words sank in.

"Some people don't even know that they're murderers."

"Like split personalities?"

"Exactly. They murder people, bury them, and aren't even aware of what they've done."

"Amazing. Dexter, would you say that Alfred Hitchcock's movies are realistic?"

"I wouldn't say they're documentaries, but I wouldn't rule anything out as impossible, either, Spot. There are a lot of disturbed people out there."

"Dexter, I really miss you. You don't know what it's like with you away at college." Maxwell was sorry the instant she said it. Now Dexter would think she was a baby.

"Yes, I do, Spot. I'm awfully homesick for you, too."

He hugged her.

"Can't you go to school closer to home?"

"You know I want to go to school up north. That's the one thing I'm sure of. You'll be fine, Spot. I would never have left home if I hadn't been sure of that. I've always thought of you as being self-contained. You like being alone, don't you?"

"Well, I've got my imagination, so I guess I'm never really alone." Maxwell tried to smile. "How long will you be home this time?"

"I think I'll stay about a week. I have to get back to the book store."

"Then I'll see you in the morning. I'm beat." Maxwell glanced at the pots and pans on the stove that still needed washing. "I'll finish those tomorrow, unless the elves decide to do them for me."

"All right, Spot. I think I'll turn in, too. I'll lock up."

Maxwell passed her mother on the way to her room. Joelle Parker was painting again.

"Good night, Mom," Maxwell said. She bent down to kiss her mom's forehead.

"Good night, Max. Hey, did I forget about the dishes?"

"I did most of them."

"Sorry, Sweetie," Mrs. Parker smiled sheepishly and continued to paint.

"Maybe you can wash the pots," Maxwell said, but she got the feeling she was talking to the air again.

She went upstairs to her room. Her deducing hat was on the floor where she left it. Maxwell picked it up, placed it on her Teddy bear's head, and changed into her pajamas.

After she had changed, she looked out of the window on Mulberry Avenue. Everything was quiet. The whole neighborhood was asleep, it seemed. When she was sure Dexter and her mother were in their rooms, she grabbed her hat, tiptoed downstairs, and went outside.

Maxwell closed the front door as quietly as she could and slipped across the street. The night air felt cold against her pajamas. She shivered as she opened Mrs. Cook's gate and slowly walked into the yard.

In her haste to leave the house, Maxwell had forgotten to put on her shoes. The wet grass was slippery underneath her bare feet and, before she knew what was happening, she fell into the hole she had seen Mrs. Cook digging earlier.

"Darn it," Maxwell muttered, climbing out and trying to wipe pieces of wet grass from her feet. Her feet were starting to itch. She inched warily toward the patio.

Mrs. Cook's blinds were open and Maxwell saw several boxes lying on the dining room table. She looked beyond the table, into the kitchen. More boxes, except there was a tablecloth covering them. What were they hiding? Was it Mr. Cook? Maxwell shivered.

Something appeared to be lurking in every corner of Mrs. Cook's backyard. Even the trees seemed to be closing in on her.

She heard something creak.

Maxwell felt her heart stop. Then it began to race uncontrollably. She turned and ran out of the yard.

Maxwell was sure she could have the case wrapped up soon. *The sooner, the better,* she thought.

Maxwell tiptoed across the street. As she neared her driveway, she heard heavy footsteps behind her. She looked down at the pavement and saw the shadow of a tall, foreboding figure creeping up behind her.

The shadow reached out with its long, shadowy arm and tried to touch her shoulder, but Maxwell was not about to stick around to find out what it wanted!

She tried to scream, but she could only manage a faint whimper. She bolted for the front door, but it was locked! She turned slowly, thinking of all the things she wanted to do before she died, a list that desperately needed a lot more checkmarks.

But it was only Kenneth.

"Kenny! I'm so glad to see you."

"I have that effect on women."

"Shut up! You scared me half to death. I thought you were some kind of un-sub or something."

"Well, what are you doing out this late? In your PJs, too."

Maxwell looked down at her outfit. She was wearing baggy flannel plaid shorts, a gray tee shirt and no shoes or socks. Her feet were wet and muddy.

"I had an errand to run," she said weakly.

"Oh, of course, it's only eleven thirty. That's when I usually run all of my errands in my pajamas and bare feet."

"Well, what are you doing out so late, anyway?"

"I saw you sneaking out and wondered what you could possibly be up to. But don't try to change the subject. I'm not the one who's locked out."

"Why I'm out is really of no consequence, considering that I may not be able to get back inside. What do I do now?" Maxwell sank helplessly onto the grass.

Kenneth sat down in front of her. "I'll wait with you until you—I mean—until we think of something."

Maxwell smiled at him. "Thanks, Kenny."

"So, what were you really doing?"

"You'll think it's stupid."

"Tell me anyway."

Maxwell took a deep breath. "I was spying on Mrs. Cook."

"You were spying on Mrs. Cook," Kenneth repeated. "Why?"

"I don't know, Kenneth. I just have this idea that she killed her husband and is getting ready to bury him in her backyard."

"What gave you that idea?"

"Different things. She has this weird coffee table—the kind you'd hide a corpse in. It is a well-known fact that people often hide the bodies of people whom they have murdered in coffee tables that look like trunks," Maxwell said. She knew she was exaggerating, but it was useful to state something as a "well-known-fact" and to use words like "often" and "whom" when trying to add weight to your argument.

Her words had their intended effect. Kenneth was staring at her. "Wow," he said. "That's freaky."

"Plus, she didn't want me to go into her kitchen. Then there's the blood I saw on her shirt. And you said you saw a old man at her house the day she moved in, and he's completely disappeared. I think he was her husband and she killed him. And then there are all of those books in her living room about murder. And she practically said those books are her inspiration. I'll bet she uses them for ideas and tips on how to commit the perfect murder. And last, but not least, there's the hole I saw her digging. I fell into it a while ago. It's big enough to hold a person."

Kenneth was silent for a long while. "Wow," he said again. "But that's all circumstantial evidence, Max. Besides, you can't prove that man was her husband. Don't you need dental records and things?"

"Okay, maybe. I want to be fair about this, Kenneth. A person's innocent until proven guilty, blah, blah, blah, yadda, yadda, yadda. So we have to look for clues, like dental records, or, first things first, the body. And, you may have to testify. Do you think you would recognize the man if you saw a picture of him? And how do you know about dental records, anyway?"

"Hey, you're not the only one who watches *Criminal Minds*. But seriously, Max, you're not thinking of going back over there?"

"Well, you said it yourself. I need more evidence before I can go to the police. Look, Kenneth, it makes perfect sense. Mrs. Cook may look like a sweet old lady, but she's really strong, and she's kind of moody. I have to go back."

"Hey, I'll go with you. It sounds like fun."

"It's work, Kenneth," Maxwell reminded him.

She smiled. If Kenneth went with her, it would be fun. Besides, it would be an extra body, and there was safety in numbers.

She stood up. "I have other things to worry about now. For instance, how am I going to get inside my house?"

Kenneth also stood. "Did you try the back door?"

"No, but it's locked. I saw Dexter lock it."

"Any windows open?"

"No. Wait! I might have left mine open."

Maxwell and Kenneth ran to the driveway and looked up. Just as she suspected, the window was open. Maxwell stared, dumbstruck. Her stomach felt slightly off-kilter.

"Now all we have to do is find a ladder and you're home free," Kenneth was saying.

"You don't mean I'm going to have to climb up there?" Maxwell said. "You may as well know I'm scared of heights."

"Since when?"

"Since forever, Kenny, you don't know everything about me. I have lots of layers."

Kenny chortled. "Like an onion? Well, someone has to go up there and it can't be me."

"Why not? I'll hold the ladder for you, Kenneth."

"Look, if I go up there, it would be like breaking and entering. I could go to jail, or worse, my parents could find out. Do you know how much trouble I'd be in? I wouldn't be able to get my driver's license until I was out of college, and by then I'd be too old to drive."

"Okay, okay, I get the idea, already. I suppose I'll just have to close my eyes. So, where are we going to find a ladder?"

"I think we have one. I'll go check," Kenneth said, running over to his house.

Maxwell waited for him in the driveway, trying to look as inconspicuous as possible just in case there are any police patrolling the area. Unfortunately, none drove by.

Kenneth returned with the ladder, and Maxwell helped him set it up against the Parkers' house. He held it steady as Maxwell began her climb.

"That's it, that's it. You're almost there," Kenneth encouraged. "Just one more rung and you've got it."

Maxwell opened her eyes. She had made it. She started to look down, but the queasy feeling returned, so she climbed into her room before looking down.

"Thanks for helping me, Kenny," she called softly. "You're a true friend."

"No problem. You'd have done it for me—unless it involved heights."

Maxwell waved and Kenneth took the ladder back to his backyard.

Maxwell breathed a sigh of relief. Sometimes you had to confront your fears head on. She knew it would require every ounce of courage she could summon to go back to Mrs. Cook's house.

5. The Trouble With Mermaids

"I got it, Mom," Maxwell called as she ran past Mrs. Parker on the way to the front door.

Kenneth was standing on the doorstep, holding a tennis racket in one hand and a can of tennis balls in the other.

"I'll get my racket," Maxwell said and, after fishing it out from somewhere in the closet, met him outside.

"I figured we'd walk," Kenneth said.

"Fine by me," Maxwell answered. The birds sounded cheerful and the sun felt warm and happy. To Maxwell it seemed to be a perfect day.

She practically skipped as she and Kenneth walked down the street and around the corner to Kennedy Junior High School. It took them exactly three and a half minutes.

The school looked new and clean with its neat green lawn and stately palm trees.

"Doesn't it seem weird, after coming here all of these years to play tennis, to finally be going to school here?" Maxwell asked as they crossed the parking lot and made their way to the school's front lawn.

"Now that you mention it, I guess it does."

"Scary too, in a way, Kenneth. I'm starting to think maybe I'm not ready for junior high."

"Maxwell, you're the smartest person I know, even smarter than some of the teachers, I'll bet," Kenneth said.

"I mean I don't think I'm mature enough. You said yourself, Kenneth, that your sister thinks I'm weird. They all do. I've thought about it, and I think it's because I don't know about makeup and clothes and I don't care about those things. I just like to read and play tennis and do the things that I think are fun."

"Well, what's wrong with that, if that's what you want to do?"

"I guess what I'm trying to say is that I'm not cool enough. I don't think kids who are almost thirteen whole years old like to do the things I do." Maxwell looked at Kenneth. "Do they? Be honest, Kenny."

"Most kids may not investigate. But it doesn't matter what other people do, Max. I like the same things you do. I think you and I are the same type of person. We're not ready to give up being a kid."

"Do you think that's what it is?"

"Pretty sure."

Maxwell sat down on the low concrete wall on the school's front lawn. The letters stamped into the wall spelled out the words, *John F. Kennedy Junior High School.*

She pulled her knees up and wrapped her arms around her legs. Kenneth sat down next to her. Maxwell looked around at the empty parking lot. The school was practically a ghost town. She imagined one tumbleweed rolling across the parking lot, followed by another. Suddenly, she couldn't hear the birds chirping and the sun felt blazing hot, not warm and friendly.

"Sometimes I feel like I'm the only person in the whole world who's different. Do you know what I feel like, sometimes?" Maxwell said after a while.

"No, what?"

"The Little Mermaid."

"Hey, that was a cool movie. I watched it with my little sister. That crab was funny."

"Not the one in the movie, you dodo bird, the one in the book."

"Well, I haven't read the book. What was she like?"

"She wanted to be human more than anything else, because she thought that humans had more fun than mermaids. She would go up to the surface and watch the humans, wishing she could be a part of all the fun. Plus, she heard that humans went to heaven and she thought she was missing out on something wonderful. That's how I feel at school—that I'm only watching from the surface, that I'll never really be a part of it, and that I'm missing out on something wonderful. Do you understand what I mean?"

"I think so. Well, what happened to her?"

"She sold her voice to get legs, just like she did in the movie. Except in the book, she never got her voice back. The prince ended up falling in love with some other girl who had a beautiful voice and the Little Mermaid died—she turned into sea foam. She did finally make it to heaven, after about three hundred years of doing good deeds."

"Sounds like the movie was way better. You know, if you like fairy tales, which I don't," Kenneth said. "But aren't fairy tales supposed to end with everyone living happily ever after? People aren't supposed to die alone and miserable. That's real life."

"Hum," Maxwell said, "we'll explore your descent into cynicism later, but for now, can we please focus? "

"I mean, what's the point of that story? The mermaid is supposed to end up with the prince. That's what the story is about."

"Kenneth, " Maxwell said, "stay with me. What I'm trying to say is, sometimes I think I'm a mermaid. I look pretty much like other kids, but there's something essentially different about me. I'm always watching everyone else from the outside, and I want to be a part of things, but I know that to fit in, I'd probably have to sell my soul."

Kenneth was staring at her. "So, in other words, the Little Mermaid ended up dying because she wanted to be something she wasn't, right?"

"I guess you could say that."

"She wasn't happy with herself the way she was, right?"

"Yes."

"It's not good to not be happy with yourself."

Maxwell climbed down from the wall and started walking toward the tennis courts. "I'm happy with myself, Kenneth."

"I know," Kenneth said, following her.

"I just wish I could be more like everyone else." Maxwell noticed that Kenneth looked very concerned, so she added, "I'm not going to change or do anything drastic."

"Good. I mean, look what happened to that poor mermaid. Sea foam, pond scum, it doesn't sound appealing."

Maxwell laughed, but she felt embarrassed. "Don't look so serious, Kenny. It's no big deal. Come on, did we come here to play tennis, or what?" She tossed him a tennis ball. "You get to serve first."

"Wouldn't you rather go swimming, Ariel?" he teased, catching the ball with one hand.

"For someone who doesn't like fairy tales, you sure know a lot about that movie," Maxwell told him. "But let's see if you're still laughing after the game."

"Oh, is that a challenge?"

"Yeah, it's a challenge. You're dead meat, buddy."

Maxwell and Kenneth looked at each other and raced to get the side of the court not facing the sun.

An hour later, Maxwell and Kenneth were leaving the court.

"Good game," Kenneth told Maxwell, "even if you did beat me."

Maxwell smiled. She looked at the school one last time. The next time she set foot on campus, it would be as a full-fledged student.

6. Seventh Graders Welcome

Today was seventh grade orientation at Kennedy Junior High School.

"So, you're 100 percent, absolutely, positively certain that parents are supposed to come?" Maxwell asked as Dexter started on his third waffle.

"As I told you before, Spot, I can't remember, but—"

"I don't see how you can't remember. It wasn't a hundred years ago. It wasn't even a decade ago. It was more like eight short years ago. Why this sudden, convenient lapse of short-term memory?"

"But, as I said before," Dexter continued patiently, "Mom went with me and it wasn't a big problem."

Maxwell groaned. "I don't know what to do."

"Why are you making this into such a big deal?"

"I'm not making it into a big deal—it is a big deal. Don't you remember anything at all about being a kid? I can't start junior high school looking like a moron. Heaven knows it'll come out soon enough."

"You're not a moron," Dexter said, still patient.

Maxwell waved a letter in front of Dexter's face. "It says here, as clear as a glass of prune juice, 'Parents welcome.' What does that even mean? Are they *supposed* to come? Can they come? Will they come?"

"Spot, my advice to you is to not make this a bigger deal than it is. Make a decision and go with it."

"What if what I decide isn't right? What if it's wrong and everyone laughs at me?"

"There's no right or wrong here," Dexter said. "It is what it is."

"Oh, thanks," Maxwell said. "That's helpful."

"Spot, you can't control other people's actions. If they laugh at you for no reason, they're either stupid or they have a problem, or both. Taking your mother to orientation is not a laughing matter. If people laugh at you for that, they're crazy. Just because a few people are crazy is no reason to make yourself nuts."

"Just because a few people are crazy is no reason to make yourself nuts," Maxwell muttered under her breath.

"Very good," Dexter said, "let that be your mantra."

"Well, how do I look?" Maxwell was wearing her mom's old *Les Misérables* tee shirt under a pair of blue denim overall shorts and a pair of black canvas basketball shoes with red and blue striped socks.

"Like an angel," Dexter told her.

Maxwell smiled gratefully at him and went upstairs to get her deducing hat.

She thought about Dexter's advice. He always gave sound advice. Nevertheless, Maxwell was nervous as she rode with her mother to the school.

"Try not to be too weird, Mom." Sometimes Mrs. Parker was not to be trusted. Sometimes she tinkled and sparkled entirely too much. When the other moms and teachers knew to be pastel and subdued, she was all gauze and gossamer, bells and beads.

Maxwell pulled down the visor and looked into the mirror. She took off the deducing hat and threw it on the backseat of her mother's hybrid.

"Honey, stop worrying," Mrs. Parker told her. "It'll be fine."

Maxwell and Mrs. Parker were late getting to the school. The principal had already started speaking. They found two seats toward the back of the auditorium just in time to hear her final words.

"...each student will now pick up his or her schedule and proceed to first period when the bell rings," she said, gesturing toward a table in the front of the auditorium.

Two ladies were seated behind the table. There was a sign in front of one lady that read "A-M" and one that read "N-Z" in front of the other lady.

Maxwell looked around the crowded auditorium. The seats were filled with students, but there were very few parents. She tried to locate Kenneth in the crowd, but there were too many kids.

Maxwell tried to sink further down in her seat. As usual, she had made the wrong decision.

The bell rang and Maxwell went up to the second lady to get her schedule. Then she and her mother walked across the quad to Maxwell's first period class, beginning Spanish, in room C-2.

The door was locked and several students were waiting outside the door.

"I wonder what the holdup is, Honey," Mrs. Parker said to Maxwell.

Maxwell looked at her mother. *Just stop talking to me,* she pleaded silently. Two boys in the back of the line snickered.

If she talks to me again, I know I'll die, Maxwell thought. *Let's just hope they don't know she's with me.* However, Maxwell realized she and her mom looked too much alike for there to be any doubt that they were related.

Maxwell looked around at the students. There were only six other kids. That meant that most of the class would be eighth graders. She didn't recognize any of the seventh graders in the line. All the kids from her elementary school were probably taking one of the easy, popular electives, like graphic art or woodshop. Maxwell almost wished she had chosen an easy, popular elective, but no, she had to be global and try to learn a second language.

They had been waiting in the hallway for several minutes when the vice-principal came to unlock the room.

"You can wait inside until the next bell rings," he told the assembled students and Mrs. Parker. "That will be in a few minutes. Mrs. Carmichael called in sick today, but she should be here Monday for class." He turned the lights on and left the room.

The students filed into the classroom. Mrs. Parker walked right up to the front, and said, "Let's sit here, Sweetie. I read that teachers give the best grades to students who sit in the front rows."

"Mother, be quiet," Maxwell whispered, but it was too late. Mrs. Parker had spoken and Maxwell was certain the kids heard. Now everyone would think she was a teacher's pet wannabe.

Maxwell heard laughter from the back of the room. She had a strange feeling that those two boys from the back of the line were laughing at her. She slid down a few inches in her seat and kept repeating to herself, *Make Mom disappear. Make Mom disappear.* Then, feeling guilty, she turned to her mother and smiled. Mrs. Parker smiled back and this made Maxwell feel even worse.

I am a horrible person, she thought. *I have absolutely no redeeming qualities.*

The bell rang and Maxwell and Mrs. Parker went to second period. Social studies.

Mrs. McQueen told the students to find a seat anywhere in the classroom and she began her speech by thanking the few parents who had come for coming. Maxwell stared at the ceiling.

Besides Mrs. Parker, there were only two other parents in the room—a small, concerned-looking mother who kept asking her sickly-looking son if he could breathe and a tall businessman type in a dark suit who kept his eyes and fingers fixed on his smart phone. He seemed to be checking his e-mail. Maxwell couldn't say for sure which kid belonged to him, but she guessed it was the well-dressed girl toward the back who was busy using a sleek, expensive-looking smart phone to text someone.

Mrs. McQueen went on and on about how commendable it was for parents to show an interest in his or her child's academic progress.

"What kind of nerds would bring their mommies to school?" a voice behind Maxwell whispered. Someone laughed.

This time Maxwell wished *she* could disappear. She happened to catch Kenneth looking at her from across the room. He made a face and mouthed the words, "When's lunch?"

"Who knows," Maxwell mouthed back. "I could eat a horse."

Kenneth laughed quietly, and Maxwell felt a little better.

Maxwell's next class was science. Most of the kids from social studies were in her science class. By now, they all knew each other and were talking and laughing as if they had been friends since pre-school. Maxwell sat in the back of the classroom with her mother and watched.

Fourth period was math. Algebra I. Algebra I was ten times worse than Spanish because there were only two seventh graders besides Maxwell in the class. The class was almost entirely eighth grade, Mr. Turnkey, the teacher, told Mrs. Parker.

Mrs. Parker turned to Maxwell and smiled broadly. "Good job, Honey," she said.

Please, Maxwell begged silently, *make her stop.*

"Well, I think that went well," Mrs. Parker said as they drove home.

Maxwell looked at her mother. 'Yeah,' she wanted to say, 'compared to a root canal,' but she only sighed and stared out of the window.

As soon as she got home, Dexter asked how it went.

"Lousy," Maxwell answered.

"What do you mean lousy?"

"Lousy, in the sense that it was horrible, abominable, disgusting, and contemptible. Maybe lousy has some variant, obscure meaning in your perfect world, but that's the only meaning I'm aware of, Mr. Sexy Dexy!" Maxwell was surprised at how loud and shrill her voice sounded and how long it seemed to echo.

Following Maxwell's outburst was what seemed like an hour-long silence.

"Sexy Dexy? Excuse me, but where did you hear that term?" Dexter finally said.

"Why don't you leave me alone?" Maxwell said, ignoring his question. "This is all your fault, Dexter. You said Mom's going to orientation would be no big deal, but it was a big deal. Everyone laughed at me. They called me a nerd, Dex. School hasn't even started yet, but everyone in seventh grade already knows I'm a nerd, and it's all your fault!" Maxwell burst into tears and ran to her room.

She flung herself across her bed and sobbed. Maxwell could hear Dexter's footsteps on the stairs, getting closer and closer, until they finally stopped outside her room.

He knocked on the door.

"Go away," Maxwell called in a muffled voice.

"No, Spot, I won't. I need to talk to you. It's urgent."

"Fine, then. Come in, if you must."

Dexter came in and sat on the edge of Maxwell's bed. Maxwell sat up and wiped her eyes. They felt hot and puffy. Dexter looked at her for a long time before he spoke.

"Spot," he said finally, "I don't know what happened today, but I'm sorry about it, especially if it was my fault."

"It wasn't your fault." Maxwell looked at the floor. "It's my fault because I'm so stupid. I always do the wrong thing."

"Hey, you take that back. I won't have anyone talking about my Spot like that." Dexter put his hand under her chin and lifted her face toward him. "I love you, Spot. And I think you are a terrific person who is NOT—do you hear me? —NOT a nerd."

"But sometimes I wish I wasn't me. I wish I could be someone else."

"And the world would never know the real Maxwell Parker, and that would be a crime."

Maxwell's eyes filled with tears again.

"It's hard not to be like everyone else, Spot. People are always trying to force everyone to be just alike. If you don't fit the mold, it makes people nervous, as if you're rejecting them because maybe there's something not quite right with them. But it's their own insecurity that makes them feel that way. They don't understand that variety is what makes life interesting.

You, Maxwell "Spot" Parker, are one of the most unique and interesting people I know."

"I'm a nerd."

"Stop saying that. Anyway, what's wrong with being a nerd? When I was your age, all I wanted was to fit in. I did things I was uncomfortable with just to fit in. Believe me, I'd have been better off being a nerd."

"What kind of things did you do, Dex?"

"Whoa, Nellie. Isn't there some kind of law about not having to incriminate yourself? Anyway, that's not the important part of the story. What is important is for you to realize that when you conform, you're taking the easy way out. It takes courage to be true to yourself, Spot. Nobody wants to be unpopular. But you'll find out, there are worse things than not fitting in."

Maxwell hugged Dexter. "I've made a conclusive decision," she told him.

Dexter looked surprised.

"I've decided you're going to make an excellent psychologist."

"It's conclusive, is it?" Dexter said, laughing. "I'll keep that in mind."

Dexter went back downstairs, and Maxwell reflected on the one thing that had gone right that day. At least she hadn't worn her deducing hat to class.

7. The First Day of School

As soon as Maxwell woke up, she knew her first day of school was going to be a disaster.

First of all, she was late. Then, she couldn't find anything to wear. The outfit she picked out the night before looked too sixth grade to wear for her first day of junior high school. Then, when she finally made it downstairs—after three changes of clothes—she discovered that Dexter had left for the Bay Area.

"Mom," she wailed, "he didn't even say good-bye."

"I know, Honey, but his boss called late last night, after you had gone to bed. It was an emergency—Dexter had to fill in for another employee, so he left early this morning. He said he'll call you after school."

"But I needed him for moral support," Maxwell muttered. She was too upset to eat the French toast her mother made for her. She felt like she might be sick.

According to the clock on the microwave, it was 7:28, which meant Maxwell had just enough time to make it to the school by 7:33 if she walked. Besides, if she walked, her mom wouldn't be tempted to try to kiss her goodbye in front of everyone.

As Maxwell neared the school, she sensed that something was terribly wrong. Everything was much too quiet. There weren't any cars driving up to drop students off at the school, and the quad was completely empty, as if there had been an alien invasion and everyone on the planet except Maxwell had been taken back to the mother ship.

Maxwell looked at her watch. Seven thirty-seven. How could she be four minutes late? Why had it taken longer than three and a half minutes to walk to school, today of all days?

Maxwell wanted to turn around and go home. What kind of start was this—late on the very first day of junior high? But she continued on her way to first period.

When Maxwell got to the C building where her Spanish class was, she was briefly alarmed to see that the doors to all of the classrooms in the C building were open. This was disturbing, since the room numbers were on the front of the doors, and Maxwell couldn't remember which room was C-2. She thought it was the second door on the left. Then again, maybe it was the second door on the right.

Maxwell decided to try the second door on the left because she thought she remembered lining up on that side of the corridor. When she walked in, to her relief, she realized she chose the correct room. Yes. The desks, the chairs, the chalkboards, and the maps on the wall all looked familiar.

"*Hola. ¿Cómo estas?*" a short woman with glasses and short, grayish hair called from the front of the classroom.

Everyone turned and stared at Maxwell.

Maxwell wanted to disappear. She stared back at the woman, unable to speak.

"*¿Eres tú en esta clase?*" the woman asked.

Maxwell continued to stare at her. She felt herself turning into a statue, right there, in front of everyone's eyes. It would make a good story on the news. "And now, in local news: A young girl turned into a statue today in Spanish class. Doctors believe the cause was extreme humiliation. Her family has decided to donate her body to a wax museum."

Maxwell didn't understand why this woman was insisting on speaking to her in Spanish. She couldn't understand anything she was saying.

The teacher walked over to an empty desk and motioned for Maxwell to sit down. "*Siéntate*," she said very amiably.

Maxwell walked to the desk and sat down. As she did, her knapsack fell on the floor, and its contents spilled out. She bent down to pick them up.

She thought she heard some boys laughing in the back of the classroom, and she was sure they were laughing at her clumsiness. Her ears felt hot and she wanted to cry.

"*¿Cómo esta, clase? Me llamo Señora Carmichael. Esta clase es una clase de español. ¿Tú quieres hablar en español?*"

The teacher looked expectantly at Maxwell.

Suddenly Maxwell understood what was happening. She was in the wrong classroom. Obviously, this was not beginning Spanish. Clearly, this was intermediate Spanish, in room C-3. She had chosen the wrong door!

Maxwell was about to raise her hand to tell the teacher she was in the wrong classroom when she noticed the poster of Mexico City above the teacher's desk. She remembered seeing it Friday at orientation.

Maxwell looked up at the teacher. She seemed to be waiting for Maxwell to answer her question.

"I—I don't speak Spanish," Maxwell said softly.

"No," the teacher said, almost gleefully. "No, you don't. But I am Señora Carmichael, and I am here to teach you."

Mrs. Carmichael ran back to her desk. "*Clase,* class, open your books to page five, *página cinco,*" she said. Then she called on a boy named Tony to read the introduction.

Maxwell was miserable for the rest of the period. She felt as if she made a fool of herself. As she listened to Tony read, she felt her ears grow so hot she thought they might explode. She wondered what that would look like. Suddenly, there would be a loud noise and a puff of smoke where her head used to be. The kids would look at her sadly and say, "She died of embarrassment."

After a while, Mrs. Carmichael stood up and started running around the room, grabbing objects and calling out their names in Spanish. "*Làpis... escritorio... pluma... papel...*"

When she ran out of objects, Mrs. Carmichael passed out a worksheet.

"This is for homework," she told the class. "Since you all did so well today, I will let you talk until the bell rings. But quietly!" she said.

Maxwell didn't know anyone in the class, except for an eighth grade boy named Eric, who was sitting at his desk, playing with plastic action figures.

At least I'm not the only weirdo at this school, she thought. However, instead of comforting her, this thought only depressed her.

She looked at the worksheet. There were pictures on one side and some Spanish words on the other side. Maxwell spent the next few minutes matching the words to the pictures. *Làpis*, pencil. *Carta*, map. Well, she'd learned something, anyway.

In social studies, Mrs. McQueen greeted the students by telling them she had made a permanent seating chart, and after much confusion, the students were all in their assigned seats.

Maxwell was glad Mrs. McQueen assigned the seats alphabetically, because she and Kenneth ended up sitting near each other.

Kenneth walked to science with her, but since Mr. Springfield assigned seats randomly, she and Kenneth ended up on opposite sides of the room.

Maxwell was sitting behind two girls named Darla and Christine. They looked much older than twelve years old, mainly because they were wearing so much makeup.

Angelica would approve, Maxwell thought.

Darla had her makeup kit spread out on her desk. It looked like the MAC counter at Macy's.

"Who's the cutest guy you've seen so far?" Christine asked Darla as they needlessly reapplied their lipstick.

"Oh. My. God! Kenneth Newman. He's in my first period and he's so hot. He talked to me all period, and I was like, my god, I don't even know you." Darla handed Christine an eyelash curler.

"Maybe he likes you," Christine said, as she curled her eyelashes.

Maxwell suppressed a snort. *How moronic,* she thought. She pretended to study the graffiti on her desk.

"He wouldn't be the first," Darla said, and they laughed.

Maxwell glanced over at Kenneth. He was talking to Britney and Britney's best friend, Alice. Britney was little and cute and giggled a lot. Alice, according to most of the girls in Maxwell's class, looked like a supermodel, whatever that meant.

Maxwell wondered if Kenneth would like these girls better than he liked her. Suddenly she didn't feel like laughing anymore.

"Hey." She heard a voice next to her. Maxwell turned around. A girl was holding out a folded piece of paper. Maxwell looked at it.

"Can you pass this to Chad?" the girl asked. Maxwell took the note and handed it to the boy in front of her. She watched as he opened it and read it.

Maxwell took a piece of paper from her notebook and wrote:

Dear Dexter,

I already miss you. I know you had to go back to class and everything, but I wish you didn't have to. I wish I had a friend. I hate my life. I need a friend. Please help me.

With love,

Your Spot

She folded the letter into a very small square and put it in her knapsack.

Finally, the bell rang. Maxwell walked to fourth period alone, because no one she knew was going her way.

Maxwell's fourth period class was math. Mr. Turnkey gave an assessment test. When the allotted time was up, he told the class to exchange papers with a neighbor for correction.

"I'll trade with you," said the girl sitting in front of Maxwell.

She was about Maxwell's height, with short, blonde hair, and braces. She had no folders, but carried a huge designer bag. Her name was Veronica.

After they corrected the tests, Veronica turned around. "You got a hundred," she told Maxwell. "You're smart, aren't you?"

"Well," Maxwell began, not sure how to answer her.

"I'm not very smart," Veronica continued, "especially not in math. Maybe you can help me."

"I can try." Maxwell said, but she noticed that instead of looking at her, Veronica was focusing her gaze on the hallway outside the room.

As soon as the bell rang, Veronica ran out of the room, and Maxwell could hear her calling, "Tammi, wait up," as she hurried off toward the lunch room.

Maxwell headed to the lunch room, but stopped short of the huge crowd trying to squeeze into the double doors. She didn't see anyone she knew, so she decided to go home for lunch.

Instead of eating, Maxwell went to her room and listened to a Harry Connick, Jr. song on her MP3 player.

She arrived back at school just in time to find Kenneth to walk to P.E. with him. Once they reached the P.E. area, Kenneth went to the boys' locker room and Maxwell continued on to the girls'.

Mrs. Robins, the girls' P.E. teacher, assembled the girls in the locker room and began her annual "Welcome to P.E." speech.

"We're here to play hard, girls," she said. "So I hope all of you girlie girls, and you know who you are," she said, glaring at the class, "will leave your fake nails at home." Maxwell looked at her hands. Her fingernails were a respectable length, not gnawed off, but certainly not long and curvy. Piano-playing length, she called them. She hoped Mrs. Robins wouldn't consider her a girlie girl.

Finally, Mrs. Robins dismissed the girls to the bleachers for free time, but not before reminding them to purchase their P.E. clothes after school, if they hadn't already because they would have to "dress out" the next day.

The girls filed out of the locker room and made their way to the field, amid shouts of glee, gales of laughter, and animated conversations.

So excited about nothing, Maxwell thought, glumly. She wondered what Mrs. Cook was up to.

Maxwell walked to the bleachers slowly and went straight to the top. She took her notebook out of her knapsack and jotted down some notes about her investigation.

The boys had been dismissed too, and they were off in the distance, tossing a football to one another. Kenneth was running around the field, and Maxwell happened to catch him looking her way. She smiled and waved. As he attempted to wave back, a boy named Charlie tackled him.

"Hey, hey," yelled Mr. Gillis, the boys' P.E. teacher, "this isn't touch football. No tackling. Next time, I'm giving you laps."

Maxwell chuckled and watched Kenneth dust himself off.

Her attention was diverted by a large group of girls sitting near the bottom of the bleachers. Veronica was sitting at the very edge of the group and kept straining to hear what the girls toward the middle were saying. Every so often, the group would spontaneously burst into laughter as if someone had just told the world's funniest joke. Veronica laughed along with them, even though Maxwell could tell she hadn't a clue what they were talking about.

A girl named Tammi ran to the track and started doing cartwheels and handsprings.

"Wow!...That's great, Tammi," the girls called.

One girl named Lisa ran up to Tammi and hugged her, saying: "You're going to make the cheerleading squad for sure!"

Maxwell caught Veronica looking at her. She started to wave, but Veronica quickly turned away.

When Maxwell got home, there was a message to call Dexter.

"Hey, Spot," he said when he finally came to the phone.

"What took you so long?" Maxwell asked.

"I was heating up some ramen." Maxwell could hear him slurping, so she knew he was eating it as they spoke.

"Dexter, you left and you didn't even say good-bye."

"I know, Spot, but you needed your rest."

"Dex, I want to apologize." She took a deep breath. "I was mean to you for no reason. It wasn't your fault." She started to cry. "You're the best brother in the whole world and I love you. I'm sorry about calling you Sexy Dexy. I mean, I'm sorry about listening to your phone conversation, but that was a long time ago and I only did it once."

Dexter laughed. "That's okay. I was a little surprised to hear you call me that. Angelica used to, but I made her stop. I hated it."

"Oh, good. I couldn't stand the thought of my brother being called a degrading and sexist name like that."

"Well, now you don't have to."

"I wrote you a letter today, Dexter, but I don't think I'll mail it. I feel better now, talking to you."

"Glad to be of service. You know, Spot, I saw my counselor today. It's official. I've switched my major. For better or for worse, I'm going to study psychology."

"Excellent," Maxwell said. "And don't worry, Dex, You'll be a great psychologist. And it doesn't mean you have to give up journalism completely. You can write books, and you can even have a talk show, if you want. You can be like Dr. Phil, except younger and with more hair."

Dexter laughed. "Listen, Spot, I'm here if you ever need to talk to someone—about anything. Got it?"

"Okay, Dexter."

"Take care, Spot. We'll talk soon."

"Thanks, Dexter. Love you."

Maxwell hung up. She felt funny, as if she wanted to cry, even though she wasn't sad anymore.

She heard the sound of dogs barking outside, distant at first, but the noise got progressively louder as the dogs closer to the Parkers' house joined in.

Maxwell went to the window to identify the source of the disturbance.

The only unusual thing she noticed was a teenage boy walking a gray and white miniature schnauzer down the street past her house. Both boy and dog seemed oblivious to the commotion they were causing. The boy stopped in front of Mr. Bentley's house, two doors from the Parkers. Mr. Bentley's garbage bin was out, even though garbage day wasn't for another two days. The boy lifted the lid and dumped his plastic doggie bag inside.

"That's uncalled for," Maxwell said aloud, "and totally gross."

She wondered if it was a serious enough offense to warrant a call to the police station. She decided against it, but made a mental note: Don't leave the garbage bins out when it's not garbage day or you may receive an unwelcome surprise!

8. Neighborhood Watch

He heard a sound behind him, like the dull thud of a wooden leg on synthetic tile. "Maxwell, is that you?" he called uncertainly. An arm reached up in the dark and brought a blunt instrument deftly upon his head. He tottered and fell into the potted palm.

When Maxwell returned to the penthouse, she called out the name that fell so sweetly from her lips: "Kenneth." There was no answer, so Maxwell switched on the light. Her beloved Kenneth lay on the cold, hard floor, engulfed in a pool of blood...

Maxwell put her pen down. It was almost time to go to Mrs. Cook's house.

She went downstairs. The living room was empty. Maxwell sat down on the couch and made a face. "There's nothing to do," she said aloud, but no one was there to hear her.

"If a tree falls in the forest and no one's there to hear it, does it make a sound?" she asked.

No one answered.

"I *hate* being alone!" Maxwell said, very loudly. If her mother had been home, she would have looked shocked and told Maxwell, for heaven's sake, there was no need to shout.

"Why can't we have a pet?" Maxwell said, again, to no one in particular. At least a pet would listen to her. If it was a parrot, it might even answer back.

Maxwell wished she had gone to the art show with her mother.

The doorbell rang.

"Are you busy?" Kenneth asked when Maxwell opened the door.

She shook her head.

"I saw Mrs. Cook leave. I think she went to the grocery store. Now's our chance, Max. Get a jacket and let's go."

Kenneth was wearing jeans, a white tee shirt and a black bomber jacket. Maxwell thought he looked just like an airplane pilot, except he didn't have a scarf thrown casually around his neck. Maybe after they took Mrs. Cook "downtown," where she belonged, they could hop on a plane to South America. They would go from ruin to ruin, searching for valuable artifacts and lost treasures.

Maybe the Nazis or the lackeys of some other evil dictator intent on world domination would catch on to them and try to thwart their mission, like they did in the Indiana Jones movies.

Maxwell found an old gray sweatshirt in the closet. She put it on and pushed up the sleeves with a business-like air.

"Kenneth, can you fly a plane?"

"No, but I flew to New York by myself last summer."

Maxwell thought about that for a minute. "Close enough. Just let me get a camera, and I'll meet you outside."

Maxwell got her mother's digital camcorder and joined Kenneth outside. She took a wide shot of Mrs. Cook's house. The street was empty, except for a white carpet cleaning van parked down the street.

"What's that van doing there? It's ruining my shot," Maxwell complained.

"That and the fact that tomorrow's garbage day," Kenneth said.

"That reminds me. I saw the weirdest thing, the other day. This kid was walking his dog and dumped the doggie doo-doo bag in Mr. Bentley's garbage bin."

"What's weird about that? Garbage is garbage."

"Well, it wasn't Mr. Bentley's garbage. What's so hard about taking your yucky trash home with you and disposing of it in your own garbage bin?"

"Maybe he didn't want to carry a stinky bag all the way home."

"You have an answer for everything," Maxwell said.

She was annoyed that Kenny wanted to make excuses for the gross polluter. Maybe it was a guy thing.

The night was dark and unusually quiet. The clouds were obscuring the full moon, which cast an eerie glow on the night.

"Wait, Kenneth," Maxwell whispered, grabbing his arm. "It's spooky out here."

"Yeah, cool, isn't it?"

"Sure, if horror movies are your idea of something cool."

"Maxwell, this seems like the kind of night that would be perfect for a murder, doesn't it?"

Maxwell nodded. There was something sinister in the air. "Well," she said, gathering what courage she could, "we might as well get it over with."

"So, what's our plan?"

"We're looking for something that will prove she killed her husband. Pictures, blood samples, you know, hard evidence—cold facts. Maybe we can find out what she's burying in the hole."

Maxwell and Kenneth walked across the street. Maxwell filmed Kenneth as he unlatched the gate. He smiled and waved at the camera.

"Cut it out, Kenny. This is serious." *He looks adorable, though*, she thought.

As they tiptoed into the backyard, Maxwell pointed out the hole.

Kenneth shined his flashlight into the hole while Maxwell filmed.

Maxwell walked over to the living room window and panned the house with her camera. Kenneth joined her at the window.

"Kenny, stop breathing—"

"I'll die," Kenneth said.

"—on me, Kenneth. Stop breathing on me. Please, back away."

"Fine," he said, and Maxwell could tell he was offended.

Big baby, she thought. She sighed and stepped away from the house.

"What are you doing now, Max?"

"If you must know, I'm setting up an exterior shot of the house. I'd really like to get some interior shots, too. You know, I'll bet there's a picture of the elusive, late Mr. Cook somewhere in there. That would help you identify him, don't you think?"

"You're not thinking of breaking in, are you?"

"Of course not, Kenneth. That would be illegal."

"I know. But I never know, with you."

"Any evidence obtained illegally is inadmissible. For heaven's sake, Kenny, even an idiot would know that."

"Well, you don't have to be rude about it," Kenneth said.

"Just stop asking me questions. You're ruining the video."

Maxwell and Kenneth went back to the hole.

"Maybe you should get inside so we can show how large it is," Maxwell said, but Kenneth wasn't paying attention to her.

He was standing very still, listening. "Did you hear that, Maxwell?"

"What?"

"That noise."

"What noise?"

"Listen."

Maxwell heard a strange sound. "It sounds like scratching," she said.

"You mean digging!" Kenneth's voice was unusually high-pitched.

The noise did sound like digging, and whoever was digging was getting increasingly earnest.

Maxwell and Kenneth looked at each other and made a mad dash for the gate. They didn't stop running until they reached Maxwell's house, where they sat down on the bench near the front door, trying to catch their breath.

"You don't think that was Mrs. Cook, do you?" Maxwell asked after a minute.

"Who else could it have been? Her dead husband?"

The thought made Maxwell's bones chill. She shivered.

"We've just got to shake it off," Kenneth said.

"Kenneth! What if I damaged the camera? What if I didn't get enough footage?"

"We'll cross that bridge when we get to it. Meanwhile, I'm not going back over there. Are you going back over there?"

"No way. At least, not tonight. I think I may just have to pay Mrs. Cook another visit. Something tells me it's not such a great idea to go sneaking around her backyard. Someone could get killed."

"Yeah, like us."

Maxwell giggled. "And that definitely wouldn't do."

"No, I guess not. Hey, Max, remember the time you told me that you were positive that the lunch duty lady was poisoning the cafeteria's lunches?"

"That was in third grade."

"I know, but remember how we sneaked out of class and hid in the cafeteria to see if we could catch her in the act?"

"Yes, I remember."

"That was fun."

"It was, wasn't it?"

"What made you suspect her, anyway?"

"Because she was so mean and she wouldn't let us go to recess unless she personally excused us. One day I noticed she would especially make sure everyone had eaten the peas. I thought there had to be a reason, so I inspected them very carefully, and I noticed that mine had these little white granules on the top. Naturally, I assumed it was poison. I tried to warn

Curtis Berry, who was sitting in front of me, but Mrs. Murphy yelled at me to stop talking. That was highly suspicious."

"I'll say."

"After that, I was determined not to eat my peas. I hated peas and I didn't want my life cut short simply because some cafeteria Nazi forced me to eat poisoned peas."

"So, what did you do?"

"Well, I hid them in my empty milk carton when Mrs. Murphy wasn't looking. When I asked to be excused she had to let me go because my lunch tray was completely empty. Then I went to find you and told you what I suspected."

"Max, I don't know how you discover these things. I mean, I would have never noticed the poison."

"I suppose I just have a nose for crime. It makes me sick to think that Mrs. Murphy might have gotten away with her crime, but no one would believe us because we were just kids. We presented good solid evidence. They could have, at least, tested the peas. But, given a choice, people always take the adult's side."

"Do you remember how mad your mom was when the principal called to tell her we had been sneaking around the cafeteria when we were supposed to be in class?"

"Yes, she still brings it up. I guess my past will always haunt me."

As if on cue, Mrs. Parker pulled her car into the driveway. She got out of her car and walked up to the house. "Hi, kids," she called as she unlocked the front door.

"Hello, Mrs. Parker," Kenneth said.

"What have we been up to this evening?" Mrs. Parker asked.

"Nothing," Maxwell said sullenly.

"Great. So, I trust I won't be hearing about any shenanigans involving Mrs. Cook," Mrs. Parker said.

"That would be affirmative," Maxwell said quietly as Mrs. Parker went inside.

"What? What was that about?" Kenneth asked.

"She's forbidden me from investigating Mrs. Cook."

"Well, that doesn't mean we can't investigate. It just means we can't get caught, right?"

"There's a bit more to it than that," Maxwell said. "She has a way of finding things out. There are too many factors beyond my control. I say it's best to exercise extreme caution, Kenny. Otherwise there'll be heck to pay."

"Well, I'd better go home," Kenneth said, standing up. "I'll see you tomorrow, Max."

"What were you and Kenneth up to?" Mrs. Parker asked when Maxwell entered the kitchen.

"Oh, we were just talking," Maxwell said. There was no need to divulge information that would upset her mother unnecessarily, especially when she was so close to solving the murder.

9. Swifter, Higher, Stronger

The weeks rolled by and soon Maxwell, Kenneth, and the rest of the seventh graders felt as if they'd been in junior high all along.

Maxwell wanted to make Dexter proud of her, but trying to implement his advice to 'just be herself' was proving to be easier said than done. In junior high being popular was the ultimate goal, and the real Maxwell Parker was about as popular as toenail fungus. The only two people who gave her the time of day were Kenneth, of course, and Veronica, who usually had something to say to Maxwell just before she asked for help with her homework.

It was Friday and Maxwell had just reported to P.E.

Mr. Gillis was giving the seventh graders a physical fitness test in the weight room. The boys were sitting on one side of the room and the girls were sitting on the other.

Maxwell was one of the last people to enter the room. She noticed a group of girls sitting on the floor beside one of the weight machines.

Should I sit with them? Maxwell wondered. They didn't look very inviting.

Then Maxwell noticed a girl named Maria Ramsdell sitting on a bench. Maxwell was debating whether or not to join her when another girl took the last space on the bench, and the two girls started talking. Joining them would be awkward, so Maxwell sat down on the floor alone.

Thankfully, Mr. Gillis started calling for students to take their turn doing pull-ups at the bar. When Mr. Gillis called Kenneth's name, a hush fell over the girls' side of the room.

"Wow!" Alice said, as Kenneth completed his sixtieth pull-up. "How can he do so many?"

"Well, you know he takes gymnastics," Britney said.

No, he doesn't, Maxwell wanted to tell them, but she kept quiet.

"I think gymnasts have the best bodies of all athletes because they're solid muscle," Christine told the group.

"And Kenneth Newman has the best body at this school," Darla declared.

Maxwell looked at Kenneth.

Kenneth Newman wasn't a gymnast. The very thought made Maxwell want to scoff out loud.

I scoff at you, she mentally told Britney, and somehow that made her feel better.

A gymnast? Oh, please. Maxwell scoffed again, although, in those sweatpants and plain white tee shirt, he did sort of resemble one of the guys on the Olympics team. Come to think of it, Kenny was athletic, so what would prevent him from making the US men's gymnastics team, if he set his mind to it?

Absolutely nothing!

In the back of her mind, Maxwell could hear the Olympics theme song playing softly along with the drone of an announcer's voice:

"Next up, on the high bar is Kenneth Milton Newman. Kenneth Newman is a twenty-year-old from Riverdale, California. He's been on the US team for the past three years. It's an amazing story. He took up gymnastics at the age of twelve at the suggestion of his best friend, Maxwell Parker. He's made rapid progress, and the rest is history. He placed first at the US championships this year, and he's the favorite for gold at these Olympic Games. Let's watch his routine. Incidentally, Maxwell Parker is in the audience today, rooting for him, of course. Sources close to the couple say they are engaged..."

"You're up, Parker!"

That's odd, Maxwell thought, *I'm not competing in this Olympics...*

"It's your turn, Max," she heard Kenneth whisper as he walked past her on his way back to his seat.

Maxwell shook her head. Everyone in the weight room was looking at her. Mr. Gillis was standing in front of the bar, impatiently tapping his clipboard.

"Any day now, Parker," he said.

Maxwell caught Kenneth's eye and gave him a thumbs up signal and he waved to her.

"Did you see that?" Darla asked excitedly. "Kenneth Newman waved to me."

"Are you going to wave back?" Christine asked.

Darla waved to Kenneth and the two girls giggled.

"You are so lucky, Darla," someone said.

Why would Kenneth wave to Darla? Who was she to him, anyway? Darla and Christine seemed so certain that Kenneth was waving to Darla that Maxwell didn't know what to think.

Maxwell half-heartedly began her pulls-ups. She managed to do five before the bell rang.

"Saved by the bell, Parker," Mr. Gillis said, quite cynically.

Maxwell went to the girls' locker room to change.

When she came out, she saw Kenneth standing with Darla. They were talking, and Maxwell could only imagine what they were saying.

Darla was probably telling Kenneth what a great body he had, and Kenneth, just like a man, was probably falling for it, hook, line, and sinker.

Maxwell walked off in disgust.

She was waiting to get to her locker later that day when Veronica approached her.

"Maxwell, I need help with my homework. Do you think you can help me?"

"Can you come over tonight?"

"I have an orthodontist appointment after school."

"Okay, what about Saturday?" Maxwell asked, even though she had already finished her assignment and hadn't planned on thinking about algebra over the weekend.

"Well, I was thinking about—maybe—on Monday—during class—before we correct it."

"It's a long assignment, Veronica. That won't give us enough time."

"Well, I can't come to your house this weekend. I'm going to be busy. I have that appointment today, then we're going to the movies on Saturday, and the party's on Sunday," Veronica said. "Are you going to the party?"

Maxwell opened her locker. "I'm going to be busy Sunday."

"So, can you help me, Maxwell?" Veronica hesitated. "Why don't you come to the movies with us tomorrow?"

Maxwell smiled. "Okay," she said, "what are you going to see?"

Veronica told Maxwell they would decide at the theater, and told her when and where to meet her. "Then, you will help me?" she asked again before leaving.

10. At the Movies

The next day, Maxwell saw Veronica in front of the theater with a group of about five other girls. The only girls Maxwell recognized were Sabrina, Kenneth's sister, and Tammi, Veronica's friend.

Maxwell remembered how Kenneth told her that Sabrina and her friends thought she was strange. For a split second, she wanted to turn around and go back home.

She told herself to think about Indiana Jones. Would he let these girls intimidate him?

Maxwell joined the girls. "Hello," she said.

"Hi," Veronica said, uncertainly, looking at Tammi.

Tammi, Sabrina and the other girls were too busy looking at Maxwell to say anything.

"So, what are we going to see?" Maxwell asked. No one answered.

"Who invited her?" she heard one of the girls mumble.

Maxwell looked at the ground. A piece of grass was growing through the crack in the sidewalk. She kicked it with the toe of her basketball shoe.

Maxwell looked around at the girls. What was so great about them, anyway? What was the big deal? Aside from the fact that they were all dressed alike, nothing about them stood out.

The girls bought tickets to the latest Disney/Pixar cartoon, and went inside.

"Hey, remember the last time we went to the movies together?" one of the girls asked.

"Yeah, we went to see *Slasher Bash*. That was so cool."

"Isn't that rated R?" Maxwell asked.

"Of course it is—that's what made it cool. It was Tammi's idea. We paid for some dumb cartoon, but as soon as the lights went out and the usher left, we sneaked into another theater."

"It was so fun. Let's do it again," Tammi suggested. "It's perfect. *Slasher Bash II* is playing."

Everyone agreed, but Maxwell was quiet. She knew her mother wouldn't approve. Besides, they could all get in trouble if someone caught them.

"*Nobody wants to be unpopular. But you'll find out, it's worse to not be yourself,*" she could hear Dexter's voice ringing in her ears.

"I kind of want to see the cartoon," Maxwell said quietly, but no one was listening. They had already started to file into the theater.

She followed the girls into the theater. They found seats in the back, and as soon as the lights dimmed, the girl sitting next to Maxwell whispered, "Get ready. We're going to leave as soon as it starts."

Maxwell slid down in her chair. She only had a few seconds to formulate her plan. She thought so hard she missed the previews.

"Come on," the girl whispered. "We're ready."

Maxwell got up and left with the other girls. She was about to follow them into *Slasher Bash II,* when she turned to Veronica.

"I'm going to get a soda," Maxwell told her.

Veronica seemed surprised to see that Maxwell was still there. "Oh. Okay." She shrugged and followed Tammi and Sabrina into the theater.

Maxwell went into the restroom and found an empty stall where she could wait while she figured out what to do.

How weird would it look if I just left? Maxwell thought. *Then again, how weird is it that I'm hiding in the restroom? Okay. They can't force me to do something I think is wrong. I have options. I can always go home.*

Maxwell opened the door of her stall and was about to leave when the door to the restroom opened. Tammi and Sabrina came in.

Maxwell closed the door before they saw her.

"Where did that girl go?" Tammi asked.

"Who? Maxwell?"

"I don't know. Veronica's friend. Whatever her name is. What happened to her?"

"She told Veronica she was getting a soda, but I bet she went home. She's so un-cool."

"Who invited her, anyway?"

"I don't know. I know I didn't," Sabrina said. "She's just one of my brother's lame friends."

"Yeah, but you know, your brother's starting to outgrow his lameness."

"Shut up, Tammi, you don't have to live with him."

Maxwell heard Tammi and Sabrina leave the restroom. She came out of the stall. She thought about going in to finish watching *Slasher Bash II* to prove to Tammi and Sabrina that she wasn't lame.

Maxwell decided she would rather go home.

Who needs Slasher Bash II when you're living across the street from a homicidal maniac? she asked herself.

11. Party Animal

"Maxwell, would you please close the door? You're letting mosquitoes in."

"Okay, Mom," Maxwell called, not moving a muscle.

She was sitting in the doorway of the patio door. She was sitting there because the breeze felt good and because she needed to think.

Her mother was right, though. She was letting mosquitoes in. Maxwell didn't care about that, however. She had other problems to deal with, problems bigger than a few miserable blood-sucking bugs.

Sure, mosquitoes were annoying and sometimes carried diseases, like dengue, malaria, or West Nile virus. With Maxwell's luck, a mosquito carrying a rare but deadly disease would probably land on her and give her one of those rare, deadly diseases and she would die. If she did, it wouldn't matter. No one would even notice. She didn't count at all. The party was tonight, and everyone was invited, everyone except her.

Kenneth was invited. Maxwell knew this because she had just called his house and his little sister, Amy Lynn, had answered the phone and said, "Kenneth isn't home. He went to the party," as if Maxwell was supposed to know all about the party. Amy Lynn was only five and slightly ignorant when it came to things like parties.

Maxwell was angry with Kenneth for going to the party, especially when he hadn't even mentioned it to her.

"The stupid pleasure seeker," she mumbled. Yes, that was Kenneth's problem—he was a party animal. He was probably flirting, or dancing with Darla or Britney this very minute. On second thought, he was probably dancing with Darla *and* Britney this very minute. They were probably making what one of them would laughingly call a "Kenneth sandwich."

"Go, Kenneth! Go Kenneth!" they'd chant, and he'd be wearing one of those moronic expressions people always wore when they were having fun.

Grinning like a fool, Maxwell thought, gloomily.

Maxwell wondered if she should have sneaked into the movie with Veronica after all. Maybe they would have invited her to the party if she had.

She frowned.

"Maxwell, did you close the door, like I asked?" her mother called.

Maxwell got up and closed the door.

"Yes, Mother."

Maxwell went into the den. Mrs. Parker was painting. Maxwell stood and watched. Mrs. Parker continued to paint. Maxwell left the room.

She went to the piano and played chopsticks.

That got boring, so she tried improvising.

She played for almost an hour. Then she went back to the den and turned on the computer.

She went online and searched her name in Google. The only hit she got was for a company in Bismarck that marketed cleaning supplies. The company was named after its two founders, Mitchell Maxwell and Jonathan Parker. They were both thirty-five years old and had known each other since high school. Maxwell felt almost famous when she saw her name in print.

She was about to log off when a headline caught her eye.

"Backstreet Bandits Still At Large in Riverdale."

Maxwell clicked on the story.

"A credit card ring, known by police as the Backstreet Bandits, is thought to be responsible for a string of cyber crimes in Hollywood. According to an LAPD spokesman, it appears the gang is moving east, toward the Inland Empire. The young men are thought to comb suburban neighborhoods on garbage day, looking for discarded bills and other items they can use to steal the identities of local residents. Please be on the lookout for any suspicious activities in your neighborhood."

"Hum," Maxwell said. "Something interesting is happening in the IE. Finally." She read the blurb again.

"Speaking of suspicious activities, I have some footage to watch." Maxwell clicked on the video file she uploaded the last time she and Kenneth spied on Mrs. Cook's house.

She was surprised at how good the footage came out. At least now she knew her mom's camcorder took pretty good footage in low-light settings.

Maxwell imported the footage into her moviemaker software and practiced editing shots. It might make an interesting movie, after all. "The Murderer Across the Street," she typed as the title. "Directed by Maxwell Parker. Featuring Kenneth Newman." She changed the font to 'Rockwell' and made it scroll. It looked very professional.

She realized the footage wouldn't prove Mrs. Cook's guilt. To get something really useful, she would have to put Mrs. Cook's house under surveillance.

Maxwell closed her programs down and turned the computer off.

"Mom, I'm bored. Can't we do something tonight?"

Mrs. Parker looked up from the house she was painting. "What do you have in mind?"

"Can we go out to dinner?"

"Dinner?" Mrs. Parker smiled. "Why not? We haven't done that in a long time."

"We could go to The Cherry Blossom," Maxwell suggested.

As soon as Maxwell and her mother walked into the restaurant, Kim, the hostess, greeted them. "Good evening, Mrs. Parker. Hey, Maxwell. Good to see you both again."

Maxwell ordered her favorite type of sushi, spicy tuna. Her mother ordered sashimi and miso soup, and they both had green tea ice cream for dessert.

She was pouring the last of the tea when a large group of boys—eighth graders from her math class—walked into the restaurant and were seated at the table next to Maxwell and her mother.

Maxwell groaned.

"What's the matter?"

"I know these people," she whispered. "They go to my school."

"Why don't you speak to them?" Mrs. Parker asked.

"I don't know them, know them," Maxwell answered. "They're just in one of my classes."

"I see."

"No, you don't. I wish we hadn't come here."

"You love The Cherry Blossom. It's your favorite restaurant."

"It used to be."

Mrs. Parker looked concerned, so Maxwell tried to smile.

"Well, I'm glad I let you talk me into coming here. My meal was great. How was yours?"

Maxwell was about to answer her mother, when the boys at the next table laughed. They probably found it hilarious that her own mother had to be talked into spending an evening with her. Maxwell silently berated her mother for her unfortunate choice of words.

"Can we go, already?" she asked quietly.

"But you haven't finished your ice cream, Dear." Mrs. Parker sounded like she was speaking to a preschooler who didn't understand English very well.

"I am finished. Can we go?"

"Just let me finish my tea."

Maxwell forced herself not to look at the boys' table while she waited for her mother to drink her tea. It seemed like hours before her mother raised the cup to her lips. Time-lapse photography was faster than her mother drinking tea. Maxwell could almost hear each frame advance—lift, lift, lift, lift, sip, sip, sip, sip, swallow, swallow, swallow, swallow.

Her mother was in the middle of one of her slow-motion sips when the boys' table erupted with laughter again, and one of them said, "I died when he said, 'Let me just explain, Baby,' and she slammed the door in his face. It was too cold."

Maxwell smiled. They were laughing about a movie, not at her. They probably hadn't even seen her. She had never been so happy to be invisible.

Maxwell went up to her room as soon as she got home. She planned to read before going to bed. As she passed her window, she stopped to look out at Mrs. Cook's house.

A cat was walking toward the backyard. Maxwell watched as it climbed the fence and landed in the backyard. The cat sniffed around the yard. Finally, it stopped and started to dig.

Maxwell took her notebook from her knapsack. She opened it to a blank page and wrote:

Case 0632—10:00 p.m. The cat walks at midnight. Mrs. Cook's estate, shrouded in a cloud of fog, looks as dead as a tomb. A frantic feline is roaming the grounds. Could she be searching for her lost kittens—the latest in a line of innocent victims robbed of their lives by a mad, murdering widow? Will that evil woman stop at nothing? Will the murdering ever end? Perhaps she will not rest until every man, woman, and child, every dog and cat in the peaceful town of Riverdale is dead!

Maxwell closed her notebook and went to bed.

12. Kenneth's Choice

"Where's Mr. Springfield?" a boy named Ronny asked.

"He's not here today, and I'm your sub," answered the young woman sitting behind Mr. Springfield's desk. "What does Mr. Springfield usually have you do on Monday?"

"Well, he usually has a lesson planned, but last Friday he told us that he didn't have anything planned for Monday, and that we could have a free period," Darla answered before anyone else could.

"Is this true?" the substitute asked.

Everyone in the class nodded, everyone, except Maxwell, who was too busy reading to pay attention.

She was so busy that she didn't notice the substitute teacher tell the class they could talk quietly or the way everyone began to move their desks around the classroom into groups.

After a while, she heard someone calling her name, as if through a tunnel. She looked up and was surprised to find herself sitting at a black-countered desk surrounded by bookshelves containing jars of specimen suspended in formaldehyde. She was even more surprised to find that her desk was the only one left on her side of the room.

Kenneth was standing in front of her. "Earth to Maxwell," he was saying. "What are you doing?"

She held up her book. "I'm reading."

"I mean, why aren't you talking? You don't have to work today, thanks to Darla."

"I suppose some of us have a lot to be grateful to Darla for."

"What? Is something wrong?" Kenneth looked so genuinely concerned that Maxwell couldn't stay mad at him.

"No, nothing's wrong."

"Good. Now, about Mrs. Cook—I've noticed something about her. Did you know she leaves the house every Friday at about 5:00? Do you think it means anything?"

"It could. Maybe she goes out every Friday at that time to commit a murder. Maybe she's not only psychotic, maybe she's also compulsive. I'm proud of you, Kenny. You're developing a nose for crime, after all."

"Yeah, well, it's just something I noticed. Have you been by to see her? We still need some shots from inside the house."

"I know." Maxwell hadn't been able to bring herself to visit Mrs. Cook. She felt it would be phony to visit Mrs. Cook while she was the subject of her murder investigation.

"When are we going to go back over there?"

"Soon," Maxwell assured him. "We just have to make sure the time is right. So, maybe we'll go this Friday when we know she won't be there."

"All right, it's a date."

"I called you last night, but you weren't home." As soon as Maxwell said it, she was sorry.

"I know, I went to this party last night—" Kenneth was about to say more when Britney came over.

"Hey, Kenneth, aren't you coming back to your seat?"

"In a minute," he told Britney.

"Don't let me keep you," Maxwell said after Britney returned to her seat.

"As I was saying," Kenneth continued, "I went to this party last night. It was so lame. There were a lot of girls there and there was dancing. You were smart not to go, Max."

"I wasn't invited," she replied. *You big dummy,* she thought. *Now he knows you're a loser.*

"Be glad, then. The music was lame and the food was disgusting. The best part of the whole party was when Tammi's parents came in and yelled at her for having the music up too loud."

"How do you know Tammi?"

"Tammi? She's friends with Sabrina."

"Oh. Well, I'm glad you had a nice time."

"I didn't. That's what I've been trying to tell you. Weren't you listening?"

"Of course. I have excellent listening skills. I'm a natural-born listener."

"Maxwell, what's wrong? You're not acting like yourself at all."

"I would think you'd be glad about that."

"Max—" Kenneth stopped mid-sentence again because Britney was calling him. "I'll be right back," he muttered.

Go to her, Maxwell thought as Kenneth walked off. *Go to them all.*

Maxwell tried to resume reading, but she found herself watching Kenneth.

He was talking to Britney and Alice. They seemed to be enjoying themselves immensely. Britney kept touching Kenneth's hair, and they were all laughing. She hated how people were always touching Kenneth's hair because it was soft and curly. Why didn't it bother him?

Then a horrible thought occurred to her: Maybe Kenneth liked it.

Maxwell couldn't read anymore after that. She put her book away and waited for the bell to ring.

When it finally rang, she waited by her desk for the room to clear so she could talk to Kenneth alone, but Britney kept clinging to him.

Maxwell knew exactly what she would have to say to Kenneth.

"Kenneth," she would say, "I cannot tolerate the way you allow Britney to flirt with you. You've simply got to make a choice—life is full of choices—and this very well may be the most important one you'll ever have to make. So, what's it going to be, Kenneth? Will it be her or me?"

"I choose...Britney," Kenneth would say. Then he would self-destruct, just like the bad guy at the end of that Indiana Jones movie.

"He chose poorly," Maxwell would say.

Maxwell picked up her knapsack and started to leave. She certainly wasn't going to talk to Kenneth, not with Britney permanently fused to him.

In third grade, Maxwell and Kenneth stopped playing together at recess because the other kids thought it was gross for girls to play with boys, so Kenneth played basketball with the boys and Maxwell played tether ball.

Once, she'd gone over to the basketball court to tell Kenneth a joke she had just made up. The joke was too funny to wait until they got home.

"Want to hear a joke, Kenny?" she asked when it was his turn to take the ball out.

The boys whooped with laughter. "She calls him Kenny," Charlie Macabe hooted. "Is she your girlfriend, Newman?"

"Yeah, is she your girlfriend?" the other boys demanded.

"Heck, no," Kenneth had told them.

Just like that. *Heck, no.*

Maxwell still remembered how she had felt—as if someone had sucker punched her in the trachea.

Later, Kenneth had explained that he hadn't really meant it, he just didn't like the boys teasing him. Maxwell had forgiven him, but it didn't take the sting away.

Now that Kenneth was hanging around girls like Britney and Darla, Maxwell was afraid if someone asked him if Maxwell Parker was his girlfriend, he would answer the same way he had four years ago. "Heck, no," he would say. Only this time, he'd mean it.

"Max," Kenneth called.

Maxwell turned around. "What?"

Britney was watching Kenneth. She was hanging on to his every word.

Maxwell raised her eyebrows impatiently at Kenneth. She was afraid she'd done it with more attitude than she had intended.

"Never mind," Kenneth said, "I'll tell you later."

Maxwell readjusted her knapsack. "See you, Kenneth." She tried to sound bubbly and cute, like Britney, but she thought she just sounded stupid.

Maxwell felt Britney's eyes boring into her back as she left the room, staring at her with that he-likes-me-better-than-you look.

Veronica was waiting for Maxwell at the door of Mr. Turnkey's class.

"So, are you still going to help me?" Veronica asked when she saw Maxwell.

"Hello, Veronica." Why couldn't Veronica ever say hi before asking about homework?

"Are you?"

"Am I, what?"

"You said you'd help me finish my homework. Will you still?"

"Oh, yeah, sure. I just forgot, that's all."

"Oh, I thought you were mad at me—because of what happened Saturday," Veronica said as she followed Maxwell to her seat.

"What happened Saturday? Why would I be mad?"

"Well, you just left."

"Oh, that. I couldn't stay for the movie. I mean, something came up."

Veronica sighed in relief. "Good. You had me scared there, for a minute."

"Well, let's get started, Veronica." Maxwell looked at her. She was watching the kids walking past the classroom.

"Just a minute," she told Maxwell. She got up and left the room.

Maxwell watched her leave. Not only did Veronica demand that Maxwell do her a favor, she had the nerve to make Maxwell do it at her convenience.

Maxwell knew what Dexter would say about this. "Show some backbone, Spot," he'd say.

By the time Veronica returned to her seat, Maxwell was working on her assignment.

"Maxwell, help," Veronica said, turning around.

"It's too late. What were you doing out there, anyway?"

"Oh, nothing." Veronica was still looking out into the hallway. "Just talking to some people." She waved to someone. "I just have a few problems I couldn't finish. If you could just give me the answers..."

Veronica slid her paper on Maxwell's desk.

Maxwell sighed. Helping Veronica was just like pulling teeth. Maxwell wished she could get sick so she wouldn't have to come to school for a nice, long time. Just long enough to give Veronica time to find a new tutor.

Maxwell was in a bad mood when she got to English. She had eaten a bowl of vegetable soup for lunch. Eating vegetable soup always put Maxwell in a bad mood because she could never find all of the letters she needed to spell her name.

Kenneth came in shortly after Maxwell sat down.

"Hi, Maxwell. How was lunch?" he asked as he settled into his desk.

"I went home."

"Then you didn't see the new chips they have at the snack bar. They're the ones you like—you know, those jalapeno kettle chips. I saved some for you." He pulled a small bag of chips from his gym bag and handed them to her.

Maxwell smiled and put the chips in her knapsack. She took out her book.

She was just getting caught up in the story again, when Mrs. Dumas said, "Britney, please find your seat."

Maxwell looked up from her book and saw that Britney was kneeling in the middle of the aisle between Maxwell and Kenneth, talking to Kenneth. Britney's foot was on Maxwell's knapsack.

"The term 'silent reading' implies both reading and silence," Mrs. Dumas continued. "No more talking."

Britney smiled at Kenneth and went back to her seat.

Maxwell picked up her knapsack and dusted it off. She closed her book and put her head on her desk.

Mrs. Dumas came by and put her hand on Maxwell's shoulder. "Are you feeling all right?"

Maxwell looked up at her. "I have a headache. Can I rest for a little while?"

Mrs. Dumas nodded and walked off.

Maxwell put her head back down. I'm having violent mood swings, she thought. This can't be good.

13. Bugging Out

Saturday was bright and sunny, although cool. Maxwell woke up early, put on a pair of blue and gray plaid leggings and a lime green sweatshirt, and went downstairs where she found her mother staring out of the kitchen window.

"Can we make paninis for breakfast?" Maxwell asked.

Her mother turned and smiled. "Why not?"

Maxwell got the eggs, ham, and cheese, while her mother got the bread and the panini grill.

"What are your plans, today, Mom?" she asked casually.

"Hum," Mrs. Parker said absently. "I need to paint."

Good, Maxwell thought. *Her preoccupation suits my purposes.*

The paninis were hot and cheesy. Maxwell glanced at her mother over her sandwich. "Delicious," she said.

"Hum," her mother said again.

When they were finished with breakfast, Maxwell went back upstairs. She wanted to change into something a bit drabber. She changed into a black turtleneck sweater and a pair of black yoga pants. She added her fishing hat and knapsack and went downstairs.

Her mother was milling around in the den and Maxwell was able to slip outside without her noticing.

Before she got too far up the street, however, she heard Kenneth calling her.

Maxwell stopped and waited for Kenneth to catch up.

"Where are we off to?" he asked, falling in step with her.

"Well," Maxwell said deliberately, "*I* am walking to Wal-Mart."

"Okay, I'll go. What are we buying?"

"That wasn't exactly an invitation. But, if you must know, I need to buy a cell phone."

"Really?"

"Really. I need a cheap cell phone. It's something I saw on TV last night."

"I saw that, too. You're going to use it to spy on Mrs. Cook."

"You got that right."

"Coolness."

Kenneth never used to say 'coolness.' He must have picked that up from Britney or Darla.

Maxwell chuckled softly, but she was annoyed. "Are you sure?" she asked.

"About what?"

"Are you sure you want to go? I mean, is it going to be exciting enough for you? I suppose I could start giggling, or maybe I should exclaim loudly from time to time or squeal like a pig."

Kenneth looked confused. "Why would you do that?"

Maxwell stopped walking. *How can he be so oblivious?* she wondered.

Just then, a flock of geese flying overhead starting honking to one another.

"Wow," Kenneth said. "Look at them go. Awesome."

Maxwell watched the geese flying in and out of formation. The light from the sun kept bouncing off their wings as they flew. She watched Kenneth watching them. Suddenly, she forgot why she was mad at him.

"Coolness," she said under her breath.

Kenneth smiled at her. "I know, right?"

"Good job the other day with the pull-ups," Maxwell said.

"Huh?" Kenneth turned to Maxwell.

"You did more than anyone in the class. Really good job," she repeated.

"Aw, thanks, Max," Kenneth said. "Come on, I'll race you."

When they got to Wal-Mart, Kenneth led Maxwell to the electronics section and started pointing out cell phones.

"This one's cool," he said. "Look at this one!"

"Calm down. I'm just looking for a basic phone, with no bells or whistles, the simpler and cheaper, the better, since I need two."

"Well then, what about this," Kenneth handed Maxwell a boring-looking silver-colored phone with big number keys and one red key marked "end" and one green key marked "send."

"Perfect. It looks like it can't do anything but make phone calls."

"Can I help you kids with anything?" the sales clerk behind the counter finally asked. She had been talking on the phone with, from the sound of the conversation, her boyfriend.

"Nope," Maxwell said, "found it."

"Just let me know if you have any questions," she muttered and went back to her conversation.

"What's she going to do, continue to ignore us?" Maxwell whispered to Kenneth.

"I know, right?" Kenneth said laughing.

They went to the front of the store to pay for the phones and soon they were on their way home.

"So, I just have to re-jigger these, like they did last night and we'll be in business. I'll leave one of them at her house and the other one will be able to pick up anything she says. Basically, I'm creating a make-shift baby monitor."

"This is probably the coolest thing we've ever done," Kenneth said. They turned down Mulberry Avenue and approached their adjoining driveways.

"I guess here's where we part company," Maxwell told Kenneth.

"I wish I could help you plant the bug," Kenneth said.

"I know, but this is a one-man operation," Maxwell said. "If we both went, she might get suspicious." For some reason, she felt nervous.

Mrs. Newman was standing on the Newmans' front porch glaring at Kenneth.

"Oh, man, I was supposed to clean the pool before I left. I better go," Kenneth said. "Don't let anything go down without me."

"I can't make any promises, Kenny. Crime happens on its own schedule. I'm going to go fix the phone, then I'll go over to Mrs. Cook's to make the drop."

"Sounds exciting." Kenneth looked disappointed.

"I'll tell you all about it. So, go clean your pool, and I'll keep you posted."

Entering the house, Maxwell tore open one of the cell phone packages and took the cell phones into the kitchen. She found a screw driver, sat down at the kitchen counter and quickly and adeptly made a few minor adjustments to the phones.

She smiled. Then she laughed. "Mrs. Cook's not going to know what hit her," she said.

Maxwell crossed the street, marched up to Mrs. Cook's house, and resolutely knocked on the front door. She took her deducing hat off and stuffed it into her knapsack with the modified cell phone.

Mrs. Cook opened the door. "Maxwell!" she said. "Come in. Sit down. Let me get you a cup of chai." Maxwell sat down on the sofa while Mrs. Cook went to the kitchen to prepare the chai.

She returned with two steaming cups of sweet, spicy tea.

"So, how's life treating you?" she asked as she sat down in one of the flowery armchairs.

"Things are good," Maxwell said, sipping her chai. She patted her knapsack reassuringly. The cell phone was still there.

"And how's the new school? Are you adjusting to junior high?"

"It's okay," Maxwell said. "It's school."

"Well, what's your favorite subject this year?" Mrs. Cook asked.

"I like them all," Maxwell told her. "Except P.E. I'm not very athletic, when it comes to team sports, anyway. I guess I don't see the point."

Mrs. Cook laughed. "Well, it's supposed to build character. That's the standard answer, isn't it? But I suspect you're not much of a team player."

"Hum," Maxwell said. "I guess not. Is it that obvious?"

Mrs. Cook laughed again. "Would you like some brownies?" she asked.

"Yes, please," Maxwell said. She watched as Mrs. Cook returned to the kitchen. When she was safely out of sight, Maxwell carefully removed the cell phone from her knapsack and placed it under the sofa.

Mrs. Cook returned with a plate of brownies and she and Maxwell talked and ate brownies for the next few minutes.

Finally, Maxwell took her leave, explaining that she had chores to do at home.

"Come again, soon," Mrs. Cook said as she walked Maxwell to the door.

Just before she left, Maxwell looked back at the sofa. You couldn't even see the cell phone where she had stashed it. She suppressed a satisfied smile.

Later that evening, Maxwell was sitting in her room. The other cell phone lay on her nightstand. Every now and then, it would buzz with static, but so far there had been no discernible conversation. Maxwell's heart was racing. Spying on people certainly was stressful.

Then, all of a sudden, she heard Mrs. Cook's landline ringing. Maxwell felt like her heart stopped. She held her breath.

"Oh, hello Marty," Mrs. Cook said. "Yes, I'm making progress. Your research did prove helpful. I have lots to choose from in the tasteless category and a few in the odorless category. But I'm primarily interested in poisons that are both tasteless and odorless. So, you'll keep looking for me? Thanks, you're a dear. 'Bye now."

Maxwell almost fell off her bed. Mrs. Cook spoke so blatantly and casually about such things as undetectable poisons. Then again, she had no way of knowing that Maxwell was listening in.

Maxwell hoped Mrs. Cook would get another phone call, but suddenly she heard Mrs. Cook say quite loudly: "Hum. What's this? Little Maxwell must have dropped it."

She heard a rustling noise and then the phone line went dead.

"Great," Maxwell said. "That ends that."

She went to the window. Mrs. Cook was coming out of her house, silver cell phone in hand. She crossed the street and walked up to the Parkers' house. Moments later, the doorbell rang.

Maxwell heard her mother answer the door.

"No," she heard her say. "It's not mine, and Maxwell doesn't have a cell phone."

"How odd," Mrs. Cook said. "I wonder whose it could be. Maybe the plumber dropped it last week."

They exchanged a few more words that Maxwell couldn't hear. Then the door closed, and Maxwell heard her mother return to the den.

Maxwell tiptoed downstairs and slipped out into the backyard. She exited the gate and crossed over to Kenneth's backyard.

"How'd it go?" He was fishing leaves from the surface of his pool with a long-handled basket.

"Well, Mrs. Cook got a phone call from some guy named Marty and they were talking on and on about how to poison someone and not get caught."

"Wait. What?" Kenneth asked, excitedly.

"Yeah, it seems they're in cahoots. But the conversation was short and generic, almost like it was in code. And Mrs. Cook found the cell phone before I had a chance to overhear anything else useful."

"Aw, man."

"She picked it up and said, 'Oh, look, Little Maxwell must have dropped it.' Little Maxwell?"

"Well," Kenneth said looking down at her, "you are kind of short."

"Just because you're turning into a bean pole is no reason to call people names," Maxwell said.

"And calling me a bean pole doesn't count as name-calling?" Kenneth asked.

"Well, you are growing. It's a fact," Maxwell said.

"And you're not. That's a fact, too," Kenneth said, laughing.

Maxwell laughed with him. "Okay. Can we focus? Kenny, she brought the phone over and asked my mom about it, so now I'm probably going to have to field more questions from my mom."

"You can handle that," Kenneth told her. "Anyway, it seems we're on the right track."

"Yep. She's guilty, all right."

"So, we hang tight and wait for her to make a move," Kenneth said. "Right?"

"Or, a mistake," Maxwell answered. "We'll be there to catch her."

14. Group Project

"I hate this class, don't you?"

Maxwell looked up from her book. Maria Ramsdell was talking to her. Maria hardly ever said anything. In fact, she had been sitting in front of Maxwell since school began and Maxwell had never heard her speak.

"What did you say?" Maxwell asked.

"I hate this class. Mrs. McQueen is so boring."

"I know," Maxwell said, even though she did like learning about the Phoenicians and the Fertile Crescent.

"What are you reading?" Maria said.

Maxwell held her book up. "It was next on my must-read list."

"Oh." Maria looked bored.

Maxwell had forgotten that most of the girls at JFK Junior High didn't talk about books, unless the "book" was loaded with glossy photos of some teenage Hollywood hunk or the latest *celebutante*.

"Have you teamed up with anyone for the project?" Maria asked.

"No, I figured everyone already had a partner."

Mrs. McQueen was making the seventh graders do a report on a country and they had to work in groups of two or three. Kenneth had already been drafted to Team Darla and Christine and Maxwell was hoping Mrs. McQueen would let her work alone.

"I don't," Maria said. "Do you want to be partners?"

Maxwell looked at her. She seemed nice enough, but they didn't seem to have much in common. Then again, Maxwell didn't know anything about her. "Okay," she said.

"So, what country do you want to do our report on?" Maria asked.

"Greece."

"Britney is doing Greece."

"I know, but you asked which country I wanted to do."

Maria laughed. "So, what's your second choice?"

"Egypt."

"I think that's taken, too."

"Okay, Romania. I don't think anyone's taken Romania."

"No, but Howard wanted to do a report on Rome. He was very disappointed when Mrs. McQueen told him Rome is a city, not a country," Maria said.

"So dumb, and yet so popular," Maxwell said, and Maria laughed again.

Maria came over to work on the report the next day. Maxwell took her into the den so they could use the computer.

"What do you think about Kenneth Newman?" Maria asked before Maxwell could type "Romania" in the search box.

"Uh, he's my best friend."

"Do you think he's cute?"

"He's Kenny, for heaven's sake."

"Well, I think he's really, really cute."

"I'll tell him you said so."

"No, don't. I'd die."

Maxwell clicked on a website about Romania and scanned it superficially while she racked her brain for something to tell Maria.

"I was kidding," she said after a while. "I wouldn't tell him something like that. Kenny and I have far more important things to talk about than who thinks he's cute."

"Darla has a huge crush on him. She's telling everyone that he likes her, too."

"Well, Darla doesn't know him very well. And can we please talk about something else—like which of these fascinating details about Romania should end up in our report?"

"Oh, yeah, that."

Maxwell turned away from the computer screen to look at Maria. She could see she would rather talk about Kenneth.

"Did you know he lives next door?"

"You live next door to Kenneth Newman? You are so lucky." Maria's eyes had taken on a new look. Maxwell couldn't tell if it was excitement or envy.

Maxwell went to the window and raised the shade. "There's his house, right there. That window, facing us, is his bedroom."

Maria joined her at the window. "Is he at home?"

"I don't think so."

Maria sighed. "He's so nice."

Yeah, Maxwell thought, *a real prince.*

She left Maria staring out of the window and went into the kitchen. She found her mother sitting at the counter in front of the laptop. From the "cha-ching" sound it was making, Maxwell could tell she was balancing her checkbook. She was muttering under her breath, so Maxwell knew she had made a mistake somewhere and couldn't find it.

"I'll do it for you, Mom."

"I wouldn't have this problem if I didn't procrastinate. I should be more organized, like you."

Maxwell didn't feel exactly organized, at the moment. Maria's questions had left her frayed and disheveled, as if her life was on the verge of unraveling before her eyes like a poorly knitted scarf.

Maxwell pictured herself in an interrogation room and Maria was firing a battery of questions at her.

"What exactly is the nature of your relationship with Kenny? Did he ever tell you how he feels about you? How do you know he really likes you, and isn't just being nice because it's convenient? Do you really believe he doesn't know you practically worship him?"

"No," Maxwell sobbed. "It isn't true. We *are* friends. We're just friends."

"Do you expect me to believe you don't want more?"

"Are you all right?" Mrs. Parker asked. "You look ill."

Maxwell looked up. She was clutching the refrigerator door. "I'm fine, Mom. I'm just concentrating on my social studies report."

"If you're looking for something to eat, I made some more gingersnaps," Mrs. Parker said, pointing to a platter on the counter.

"Don't we have any store-bought cookies?"

"No. These are better for you. Anyway, I though you liked my cookies. I put the candied ginger in them, too."

"I like them fine. But most kids like chocolate chip. Everyone's not like us, Mom."

"Just offer them, Max. Expand her culinary horizons," Mrs. Parker said, kissing Maxwell on the top of her head. She groaned involuntarily as she turned back to her laptop.

"Mom, I said I'd do it."

"Oh, Sweetie, it occurs to me that I'm the grownup and you're the kid. Go, do some kid things. I'll be an adult for a while. It probably won't kill me."

"If you're sure," Maxwell said.

When Maxwell returned to the den, Maria was still staring out of the window at Kenneth's room.

"You're not his type," Maxwell said.

Maria turned and gave her a look. "I thought you didn't talk to him about those things."

"But, I know him. He's my friend."

"A guy can have a friend, *and* a girlfriend."

Maxwell felt as if Maria had knocked the wind out of her. She sat down on the sofa and put the plate of cookies on the coffee table.

"Would you like a cookie?" she asked weakly.

After seeing Maria out, Maxwell sat on the bench in front of her house with her mother's camcorder, surveying the neighborhood. It was her favorite hour—the one just before the sun went down. Everything was beginning to settle, as if the day knew it was almost over.

The white carpet cleaning van was parked across the street a few doors down. Maxwell was starting to think someone on the block had either started a new side business cleaning carpets or had recently discovered they were a compulsive clean-freak. No one needed to have their carpets cleaned that frequently.

Once again, Maxwell heard the familiar bustle of barking dogs and she knew, without having to look ahead, that the teenage boy and his schnauzer were approaching. Just as she suspected he would, he approached Mr. Bentley's trash can, dropped his dog waste bag inside, and hurried off.

Maxwell shook her head in disgust. She wondered if Mr. Bentley was at home. His car wasn't in the driveway, but there was a small hatchback parked in front of his house. The car had a magnetic sign on its side that said, "Mobile Geeks," so she wondered if Mr. Bentley was having networking problems. She knew he worked from home as a computer programmer. He rarely went out and never had visitors. He drove a Bentley, which Maxwell thought was an odd choice for him. He would have been better suited to a Honda or a Toyota, but his name wasn't Mr. Honda or Mr. Toyota, so in a way, it made sense.

Maxwell sometimes wondered if his name really was Mr. Bentley, or if everyone called him that because of the car.

Suddenly Mrs. Cook turned her porch light on. A few moments later, the garage door opened and Mrs. Cook got in her car. The prime suspect was on the move!

Maxwell left the camcorder on the bench and ran inside to get her skates. Her heart pounded as she took the stairs two at a time. Her skates were on the floor of her room, so she grabbed them and ran back downstairs. If she hurried, she might finally have something to report to the police.

By the time she got outside, Mrs. Cook had driven off.

Maxwell shoved her feet into her skates. She hurried to the edge of her driveway and saw Mrs. Cook making a left at the corner. Wasting no time, Maxwell skated off after her.

At first, Maxwell was able to keep up with Mrs. Cook, but as Mrs. Cook drove closer to the center of town, Maxwell kept having to stop at intersections and was unable to keep up. Besides, it was getting too dark to make anything out. Maxwell stomped the ground with her skate. "For the love of spaghetti!" she exclaimed. "She's getting away!"

Maxwell skated slowly home, rehashing the day's events. "It's obvious she was going somewhere very important in a big hurry and didn't want anyone to follow her. But, where had she gone? She could have been headed anywhere. Man, I wish I'd been able to..."

As she was about to complete her sentence, Mr. Bentley's front door opened and Mr. Bentley stepped outside. He walked over to his garbage bin and started wheeling it to the side of his house.

You're in for an unpleasant surprise, Maxwell thought. She waved to him.

"Hello, Maxwell," he said grimly.

Maxwell noticed that the Mobile Geeks car was gone. Other than that, the neighborhood looked precisely the way it had when she left. Maxwell was about to go inside, when Mrs. Cook pulled up in front of her house. She backed into her driveway, parked, got out, unlocked her front door, and went inside.

Maxwell found this highly irregular, since Mrs. Cook usually kept her car in the garage.

Just then, Mrs. Cook came out of the side gate. She looked around several times, as if to make sure no one was watching, and then walked to her car.

Maxwell crouched behind the rubber tree plant. She watched as Mrs. Cook opened the trunk and easily lifted out a large, heavy-looking sack. Maxwell strained her eyes to read the label on the bag. She gasped.

"Ready-mix cement," she said slowly.

Maxwell smiled. It almost didn't matter that she lost Mrs. Cook in the chase earlier. Every little detail wasn't important, not when you had evidence like this.

Maxwell picked up the camcorder, which she had left on the bench. "I can't believe I left it on," she muttered. She filmed

Mrs. Cook walking around to the backyard, carrying the bag of cement.

So, Mrs. Cook was going to bury the body, after all, but this time she was going to make certain no one would ever find it.

By the time Maxwell went inside, the camcorder's "low battery" warning light was flashing. "Mom's going to kill me," Maxwell said, as she plugged the camcorder into the wall.

She couldn't wait to tell Kenneth the latest about Mrs. Cook.

15. Back to School Night

Telling Kenneth would have to wait. Tonight was Back to School Night.

"Mom, hurry up. We can't be late this time, too," Maxwell said, coming into her mother's room. "You smell good," she told her. Mrs. Parker always wore the same perfume when she dressed up. Maxwell loved the woody and spicy smell. Her mom mixed it herself from essential oils.

"Thank you, Maxwell. And you look lovely."

Maxwell was wearing a vintage brick red dress with small cream-colored flowers, hiking boots, a denim jacket and, of course, her deducing hat.

"Do you really think so?" she asked, spinning around so her mother could get a better look.

"Here, have some of this." Mrs. Parker dabbed a drop of perfume behind Maxwell's ear.

"Come on, Mom. We've got to go!"

JFK Junior High looked strange at night, and there was a smell—of new basketballs, canned corn, magic markers, and paste—that Maxwell never noticed during the day. The lights in the hallways and classrooms seemed unnaturally bright.

"Mom, this is Mrs. Carmichael. Mrs. Carmichael, this is my mother, Joelle Parker."

"Pleased to meet you, Mrs. Parker. Maxwell is a joy to have in my class. She is very conscientious..."

Maxwell's mind drifted from the conversation. There was nothing more embarrassing than listening to your mom and your teacher talking about you.

Maxwell studied the other mothers in the room. Most of them were wearing various manifestations of the same velvet sweatpants and matching hoodie. The rest were wearing khaki pants with soft, light-colored blouses or tees. They all looked like they'd stepped right out of the pages of one of those catalogs with pictures of moms posing in pastel outfits and straw hats, smiling at someone off-camera, the kind of catalog her mom generally tossed in the trash without even opening. Mrs. Parker was the only mom wearing a brightly colored flowing silk tunic, jeans and sandals. She was the only mom whose earrings dangled and whose bracelets sounded like little bells.

Their hair was teased and sprayed and stayed where it was supposed to, while hers was casually tied back into a ponytail with unruly, wispy pieces that kept slipping out.

Mrs. Parker just wasn't like other people's moms. She didn't do carpools because she wouldn't remember when it was her turn. She never nagged Maxwell about her homework, not because she didn't care if Maxwell finished her homework, but because she just always seemed to know that it was done.

Maxwell noticed her mom talking to two other moms.

"Haven't seen you around, Joelle," one of them said.

"I've been busy," Mrs. Parker answered.

"Well, a bunch of us are starting a new Zumba class at the gym. You should sign up. The instructor's excellent."

"Oh, I'm not a big fan of gyms," Mrs. Parker said.

"But you must do something—you're so thin," the other mom said.

"I actually prefer hiking. There's nothing like being out there in the fresh air. It's the only time I can really think. I feel so cooped up indoors."

"Really?" one of the moms said. She looked at the other mom and the two women raised their eyebrows as if to say, "How odd."

Mrs. Parker smiled at them. She looked so happy. Maxwell looked away sadly.

On their way to Mrs. McQueen's room, Maxwell and her mother passed Mrs. Newman and Kenneth and Britney and her mother. Mrs. Newman and Britney's mom were chatting like old college roommates. Britney was telling Kenneth about a song she had just downloaded. Mrs. Parker spoke briefly, but didn't stop to talk.

Suddenly Maxwell was angry with her mother. Mrs. Parker seemed to go out of her way not to be like the other moms. Why couldn't she try just as hard to be more like them or to, at least, not be so clueless?

Maxwell was silent as she and her mother walked home. She hoped her mom would notice her silence and feel bad for ruining her evening. Maxwell could tell that her rotten mood was entirely escaping her mother's notice, because her mother kept exclaiming things like, "Would you look at those stars, Sweetie!" and "My, what a beautiful night!" Some people were so oblivious.

They went in through the kitchen, and as Mrs. Parker passed the counter, she grabbed a pile of bank statements and tossed them in the trash can.

"Good night, Angel. Sweet dreams," she said.

Maxwell went to the trash can and pulled the bank statements out.

"Mom! What do you think you're doing?"

Mrs. Parker looked startled. "What?"

"You can't just throw these away. You have to shred them. Haven't you heard of the Backstreet Bandits?"

Mrs. Parker looked confused. "No," she said. "What are you getting so worked up about?"

"There's a gang of identity thieves loose in Southern California. For all I know, they could be right here in Riverdale. Don't you watch the news? I swear, I'm not making this up," she added, because her mom was giving her that "look" again.

"Well, then, I'll trust you to take care of this for me. I'll see you in the morning."

Mrs. Parker went upstairs. Maxwell sat at the counter and stared at the stack of bank statements. Something about the conversation bothered her, but she couldn't put her finger on it.

16. Lunch Room Rules

The first four periods of the next day flew by as if they were a dream.

Maxwell nervously but resolutely approached the lunch room like a condemned sailor walking the plank. She couldn't let them see her sweat. She wouldn't give them the pleasure of seeing her becoming unglued.

The noisy clamor of kids laughing, shouting over one another, and clanking their silverware against plastic trays was periodically interrupted as the lunch lady barked out the commands: "Pick up your garbage!" or "Throw your trash in the bin!" at intervals regular enough to render them more or less expected. The din would die down for a moment or two before building back up to the same fevered pitch.

Maxwell wanted to put her hands over her ears, like little kids did when it was too loud. She looked around at the tables. Each one was like its own self-contained little world and Maxwell couldn't locate where her compatriots were hanging out. She wished she and Kenneth had been assigned the same lunch period.

She spotted Veronica with her friends at a lunch table in the center of the room. They had all bought their lunch from the à la carte menu. Maxwell looked at her brown bag and wondered if she should scrap it and buy some chili cheese fries or a hot ham and cheese sandwich to fit in with the rest of the girls. She decided she'd rather eat her almond butter and honey sandwich.

Okay, she told herself, *Operation How To Not Be Like Mom. Phase One.*

"Hello," she said, as she sat down next to Veronica. She opened her lunch bag and pulled out her sandwich.

"Oh," Veronica said, "Maxwell."

"I thought I'd try eating lunch at school, for a change," Maxwell said cheerfully, trying to ignore Veronica's less than enthusiastic greeting. She smiled at the girls around the table. They looked at each other. Some raised their eyebrows. Others shrugged.

"Anyway," Tammi said.

Maxwell waited. Apparently Tammi had been in the middle of a sentence, but she didn't continue. The girls looked at her in anticipation.

Don't say anything strange, Maxwell told herself. *Just listen and agree.*

None of the girls said anything for a long while. Finally one of them, a girl named Kayla, said: "So, like, yesterday my mom was all, 'If you don't get at least a C in math you're, like, grounded forever,' and I was like, 'Whatever.' I totally hate her. Like I'm ever going to have to use math in life."

"A lot of kids think they're never going to have to use math in real life," Maxwell said. "Actually, it'll probably come in handy more often than you'd think. For instance, if you ever have to figure out how to double a recipe or if you need to calculate a tip when you go out to dinner or if you ever get a job at some point in your life, I guarantee you you'll need the math you're learning today. Trust me, it's not a waste of time. Personally, I find it kind of fun."

"Are you some middle-age person stuck in a kid's body?" one of the girls asked and everyone laughed.

"Anyway. Parents suck," another girl said, and everyone around the table agreed.

"You should ask Angelica to help you with your homework, Kayla," Tammi said, snickering. "She's in Algebra I. How she ended up there, I'll never know."

"Only because the counselor made a mistake," Angelica said. "I suck at math, too. Maxwell's the brain. She's the one who thinks it's fun."

Everyone turned and looked at Maxwell.

"Are you a brain?" Tammi asked.

"Well," Maxwell said, "I guess I just get math, for some reason."

"Well, who cares about being good at math? It's not a skill that even matters," Tammi said. "Who cares about grades? As long as we don't get kicked off the cheerleading squad, it's all good."

"Guys don't like it if you're too smart, anyway," Sabrina said. Several of the girls nodded and exchanged knowing looks.

"What kind of guy doesn't like it if you're too smart?" Maxwell asked. "What does that even mean?"

"What does she care?" Tammi asked. "It's not like she'll ever have a real boyfriend."

"That's kind of harsh, Tam," Sabrina said, laughing and the rest of the girls giggled uneasily.

Maxwell's eyes stung. *Whatever you do, don't cry,* she repeated silently.

"Did everyone see Jonas Day's new video?" one of the girls asked and everyone started talking excitedly about the video.

Veronica turned to Maxwell. "You probably shouldn't have spoken to her," she said.

"Who? Tammi? Is she, like, your leader?" Maxwell asked.

"She just doesn't like it when people disagree with her."

"Hum," Maxwell said. "She's a dictator. I'll make a note of that."

"Good," Veronica said. Neither said anything for a while. The girls at the table continued to discuss music videos. Finally, Veronica said, "So, did you see the new video?"

"I don't usually watch videos," Maxwell said.

"Do you even know who Jonas Day is?" Veronica asked.

"Of course," Maxwell told her, annoyed. "Everyone knows who he is. I just don't really listen to him. I probably should. I'm sure he's probably very cool."

"Yeah," Veronica said, sarcastically. "Kind of. Everyone thinks so."

"For some reason, I'd rather, you know, have my own opinions about music. I like Harry Connick, Jr."

"That old guy from *Idol*?"

"He's not old," Maxwell said. "Besides, he's really talented. I mean, never mind." She could have kicked herself. Whatever happened to not saying anything weird?

"Well, whatever, we like Jonas Day," Veronica said.

"So I gather," Maxwell said. She finished her sandwich while the conversation droned on.

Someone said something about a pair of jeans on sale at the mall. Someone else exclaimed over someone else's fingernail polish. After a while, she stopped listening to the words and only listened to the tone of their voices. They sounded sing-song and hypnotic.

Maxwell smiled. *This must be the work of aliens, intent on sabotaging the human race by using female adolescent drivel to undermine society,* she thought.

"*Waw waw waw waw,*" one of the girls said.

"*Waw waw waw,*" another answered.

Maxwell looked at the clock on the wall. Five minutes until the bell.

She crumpled up her bag and stood up. She started toward the trash can, but stopped and looked at Tammi and Sabrina.

"By the way," she said sweetly, "I don't think either of you will ever have to worry about being too smart, so I'm sure you'll have lots of boyfriends."

The girls looked stunned.

"Ooh," one of them said. The rest laughed nervously. Tammi and Sabrina looked at each other, fuming.

Maxwell left the lunch room as the bell rang, smiling inside.

Operation How Not To Be Like Mom—aborted!

17. Solve For *x*

Maxwell was already in her seat when Veronica came into math class the next day. As soon as she sat down, Veronica turned around. "Maxwell, I need help."

No 'Hello,' no 'How are you?' Maxwell thought. She groaned inwardly. "What is it?" she asked.

"What's *x* in this problem?" Veronica put her paper on Maxwell's desk.

Maxwell tried to show Veronica how to solve for *x*. She hinted and prodded, but Veronica ignored all of Maxwell's hints and prods. The only thing she responded to was the answer. Maxwell finally got tired of staring at Veronica's blank face and gave her what she wanted.

Fortunately, Mr. Turnkey called the class to order with an announcement.

"Attention, everyone. I'm giving you a practice test to help you get ready for the cumulative review at the end of the month." He handed out the tests. "Now, I have to leave the room for a few minutes, so I'm putting you on the honor system. You all know the rules, and I expect you to obey them."

As soon as he left the room, Veronica turned around. "You've got to help me."

"No, she doesn't," a boy named Cameron told her. "Maxwell, don't do it."

"It's not fair if you help her," his friend George put in.

Maxwell was pretty sure George and Cameron could hear the performance her heart was putting on.

"Come on, Maxwell. Please," Veronica begged.

Why is time travel only possible in books and movies? Maxwell thought. Since she couldn't simply disappear and she couldn't say no to Veronica, she didn't exactly give Veronica the answers, but she didn't exactly make it difficult for her to copy the test.

"Aw, man," Cameron complained. "She's letting her cheat."

Maxwell wanted to die. In all of her twelve years of life, she had never cheated on anything, not even in tic-tac-toe. So much for re-creating herself as a popular girl. Veronica had given her a nice new identity as the girl who cheats on math tests.

When the bell rang, Maxwell left the classroom as fast as she could.

Later that afternoon, Kenneth came to Maxwell's house.

"Max, I wanted to ask you something," he said.

"Okay," Maxwell said. "What?"

"I heard something today at school that I couldn't believe. It was about you."

Maxwell's heart started beating fast. She thought it might explode from her chest this time.

The word was out. Someone had finally gotten around to telling Kenneth that she was a little nerdy girl with no friends and that further association with her would mean social suicide for him.

"Wh-what did you hear?" she managed to ask.

"I was talking to Cameron after school and he told me that you're in his math class and that you cheated on a test. I wouldn't have believed him, but George said it was true, too."

"Kenneth, I didn't cheat. A girl just copied my paper and I sort of let her."

"How could you, Max?"

"Lighten up, Kenny. It's not that big a deal."

Kenneth was staring at her in disbelief. "It's cheating."

"I know, Kenneth, but there was nothing else I could do. If I didn't let her copy my test, she would have gotten mad at me. She's my friend."

"I thought I was your friend."

"You are. But so is Veronica. A person can have more than one friend. You do."

"Yeah, maybe. But I don't cheat for them," Kenneth said.

It kind of annoyed Maxwell that Kenneth didn't deny having other friends. *Look at him,* she thought, *standing there all holier than thou!*

"Kenneth, would you just let it go?" she said.

"I can't, because, it's happening."

"What's happening?"

"It's happening. You're starting to sell out."

"Sell out?"

"Don't you remember what you said that day we played tennis? You said you would have to sell your soul to fit in. I never thought you really would," he said sadly.

"Well, at least I don't hang around a bunch of bimbos, like you do!"

"What are you talking about?"

"Tammi and Darla and all of those wonderful girls that you obviously like so much. And let's not forget about Britney. Why don't you go talk to Britney now, as a matter of fact, if you're so disappointed in the way I turned out?" Maxwell opened the front door.

Kenneth stared at her in disbelief. "I don't get it," he kept repeating.

"Just go home, Kenneth! I want to be alone."

"I'll go home, but I won't leave you alone."

Maxwell went up to her room and flung herself across her bed. She was angry and confused, and her head hurt.

"Mind your own business, Kenneth Newman!" she shouted.

She turned on her MP3 player and listened to a Harry Connick, Jr. song.

After a while, she fell asleep.

She imagined that Harry Connick, Jr. was on stage, singing *It Had to Be You*.

His voice trailed off halfway through the song. He shaded his eyes and looked into the audience.

"Where are you?" he called. "Is there a Maxwell Parker in the house? Will the real Maxwell Parker please stand up?"

The music stopped and a spotlight searched up and down the rows until it finally stopped on Maxwell.

Maxwell stood up and Harry Connick, Jr. looked at her. "I don't recognize you," he said. "You're changing, Maxwell Parker. How can I love you if I don't know you? Just be yourself, Maxwell. Come on, help me sing..."

Maxwell sat up in bed.

"Mind your own business, Kenneth Newman," she whispered.

18. The Wooden Shoe

When Maxwell woke up the next morning, she noticed that deep inside a peculiar feeling, a strange sense of quiet, like the calm before nature lets loose, had taken over. She wandered through periods one through three as if in a daze.

She had avoided eye-contact with Kenneth in social studies and science and, as far as she could tell, he had avoided eye-contact with her.

As soon as she walked into fourth period, she approached Mr. Turnkey.

"I need you to change my seat," she told him.

"Is there something you need to tell me?" he asked.

"Well, yes, I suppose so. There's a situation that I'm trying to avoid."

"Okay," Mr. Turnkey said. "Does this have anything to do with yesterday's practice test?"

Maxwell didn't say anything. She looked down at the floor.

Mr. Turnkey held out two practice tests. "Because I was going over these last night and I noticed something strange," he continued. "Two of my students got the exact same grade. Now, for one of them, it was no big surprise. I expected her to ace the test. But the other student seems to have made a miraculous improvement overnight."

"I didn't mean to cheat," Maxwell said. "I just didn't know how to say no."

Mr. Turnkey put the quizzes down. "Well," he said, "I'm glad you approached me, Maxwell. You know I have a zero-tolerance policy for cheaters. So, I'm giving both of you the same grade." He took his pen and marked a big red F on both papers.

Maxwell's eyes welled with tears.

"Cheer up, Kiddo. You still have an A in my class," Mr. Turnkey said. "And I have no doubt you're ready for the big test. I'll move you to the other side of the room, and we'll see how our other cheater fares."

"I'm sorry," Maxwell said. "I'm not a cheater. It won't happen again."

"I know," Mr. Turnkey told her. "And don't feel so bad. I was twelve once, too."

When Veronica came in, she looked at Maxwell's empty seat.

"Where's Maxwell?" she asked.

Cameron pointed. "She's over there."

Veronica rushed over to Maxwell's new seat. "Did Mr. Turnkey move you?" she asked.

"Yes, he did." Maxwell was surprised to hear how calm her voice sounded.

"Aw, man! Tell him you want to move back to your old seat. He'll let you. He likes you."

"I'm the one who asked to move."

"But why? I still need your help."

Maxwell took a deep breath. "But I don't need you, Veronica."

Veronica looked like a stunned deer in the path of an oncoming truck.

Maxwell felt mean, but thought it would be best to continue without stopping, like ripping off an adhesive bandage in one fell swoop. "You were just using me," she continued. "You asked me to do things for you that I would never dream of asking anyone to do for me. And I did them because I thought we were friends. But you were never my friend, and I'm not going to be able to help you cheat."

Veronica knelt down beside Maxwell's desk. "That's not true. We are friends. I liked you—I still do."

"I'm sorry, Veronica. But don't worry, I'm sure you'll find someone to fill my place." Maxwell opened her math book and started the day's assignment. "We can still be friends, if you want."

Veronica was staring at her in shock. "But—but the test," she whispered. "How am I going to pass it?"

"Let me give you a tip: study."

Veronica went back to her seat and Maxwell knew that would be the last she would see of Veronica or any of her friends.

Maxwell was in the den, later that afternoon, when she saw the light go on in Kenneth's room. She thought about calling him to tell him what happened with Veronica, but she decided he wouldn't be interested.

Maxwell went outside. Mrs. Cook's car was parked in her driveway, and Mrs. Cook was walking toward it, talking on her cell phone. She seemed flustered.

"Okay," she was saying, "I'm just leaving. I can meet you there in five minutes. Yes, The Wooden Shoe on Orange Grove. See you there." She threw a small box in the backseat of the car, climbed in the driver's side and sped off.

"The Wooden Shoe," Maxwell repeated slowly. "That's where Angelica works."

Maxwell started walking towards downtown Riverdale.

The Wooden Shoe was a European bakery and café that made delicious baked goods like sticky buns and sold homemade jams and jellies. Windmills and figurines of little boys and girls wearing clogs decorated the shop and there were small round tables topped with blue and white checked table cloths and saucy flower bouquets lining the sidewalk out front.

Mrs. Cook was sitting at one of those tables with a thin, balding man in a khaki trench coat.

The wind had picked up and it was starting to feel humid. Clouds had rolled in from the High Desert. All in all, the weather looked pretty ominous.

Maxwell found a table without being noticed by Mrs. Cook or her companion. She took her deducing hat and a large pair of sunglasses out of her knapsack and put them on. Next, she picked up the over-sized menu and hid behind it, peering over it from time to time to observe what was going on at Mrs. Cook's table.

So far, so good, she thought. Maxwell could only hope Angelica wasn't working today.

The man was looking at the contents of the box that Mrs. Cook had tossed in the back of her car.

"This is your best work yet," he said.

"The secret to it was the traceless poison," Mrs. Cook said. "Thanks for the tip."

"No problem," the man said. "I know exactly what to do with this." He gave the box a gentle pat and placed it on the empty seat next to him.

Okay, Maxwell thought. *This must be Marty. He looks shady enough.* Maxwell was dying to catch a glimpse of what was inside the box.

Just then, a Bentley pulled up and parked in front of The Wooden Shoe. Mr. Bentley got out. He sat down at a table behind Maxwell. Moments later the teenage boy with the dog approached The Wooden Shoe and joined Mr. Bentley at his table.

Oh, goodie, Maxwell thought, *we're all here.*

She ducked under the table. All it would take would be for Mr. Bentley to say 'Hello, Maxwell,' and her cover would be blown.

"Can I get you folks something to drink?" Maxwell heard a familiar voice ask.

Great! Angelica's here, too.

Maxwell strained to hear the rest of Mrs. Cook's conversation with Marty, but now Mr. Bentley and the boy were speaking in hushed tones and the two conversations were cancelling each other out.

Eventually, Maxwell's ears zeroed in on the Bentley/boy-with-a-dog conversation.

Mr. Bentley seemed to be worried about something, and oddly enough, he seemed to be speaking with a British accent.

"I told you," Mr. Bentley kept saying, but then Maxwell couldn't make out what he was supposed to have told the boy. She wondered if he was bawling the boy out for using his garbage can.

It was just getting interesting when the dog noticed Maxwell hiding under the table. He ventured over to investigate.

"Go away," she whispered, shooing him with her hand. This only made him more curious.

The boy glanced in Maxwell's direction. *Oh, dear,* she thought, *this is it.*

But the boy's focus was on the dog. "Harvey," he said in a commanding tone, and the dog returned to his feet.

Angelica came back with two glasses of mineral water. "I'll be back to take your order in a moment," she told Mr. Bentley and the boy. She was about to walk away when she noticed the dog. "Would your dog like some water?" she asked.

"That would be nice," the boy said.

Moments later Angelica returned with a bowl, which she placed on the floor beside the dog. As she did so, she noticed Maxwell crouching under the table.

"Shh," Maxwell mouthed and shook her head, but Angelica was never one for tact.

"What are you doing under there?" she asked loudly. "Get off the floor."

"I think I lost an earring," Maxwell said quietly, climbing out from under the table. "I'm fine."

"Are you here by yourself?" Angelica asked.

"Please," Maxwell said looking around. "I'll be ready to order in a minute."

Angelica walked away and Maxwell was spared, at least for the moment. She looked around the restaurant. Mrs. Cook and Marty were too busy finishing their meal to notice what was going on around them. Mr. Bentley and the teenage boy were intent on studying the menu. *Thank heaven people aren't more observant,* Maxwell thought. She turned slightly and slid down in her chair.

"Well, that was tasty," Mrs. Cook was saying. "This place has the best Dutch crust bread I've had in years."

"It's the least I could do," Marty said signing his receipt. "I'll just deduct it as a business expense, anyway." He chuckled.

"You're always thinking about the bottom-line," Mrs. Cook said.

"Which is why you hired me," Marty told her. He helped her out of her seat and the two left together.

Maxwell took her notebook out of her knapsack and wrote the following note:

Thursday, 4:30 p.m. Mrs. Cook meets "Marty" at The Wooden Shoe. The two drink coffee and have a snack. They discuss "payment" and traceless poisons. "Marty" commends her on her "best work ever."

Is Marty a hired gun? Since when do hit men file taxes?

Maxwell drew a very large question mark on the bottom of the page and closed her notebook.

"You still haven't told me what you're doing here," Angelica said.

Maxwell nearly jumped out of her seat. "You scared me half to death," she whispered.

"Why are you whispering?" Angelica whispered back.

Maxwell cleared her throat. "Sore throat," she said. "Maybe I could get some tea."

"Sure thing," Angelica said, and went back inside.

In the meantime, Mrs. Cook and Marty were getting away. Maxwell started up from her seat but, from the corner of her eye, she saw Angelica returning with a large mug. Maxwell groaned.

Well, it couldn't be helped now. She couldn't very well run after Mrs. Cook, not when she had to pay for her tea before she could leave.

Speaking of which, Maxwell remembered that she didn't have any cash with her. Not even a couple of bucks, to cover the cost of the tea, so she would have to use the credit card her mom had given her for emergencies. She'd worry about how to explain how a cup of tea at a downtown bakery constituted an emergency later.

"This was a bad idea," Mr. Bentley was saying.

"But I had to talk to you," the boy replied.

"Not here," Mr. Bentley said. "It's too public." He handed the boy an envelope. "Later," he said. He stood up and left The Wooden Shoe.

The boy stuck the envelope in his pocket then went inside to pay the bill.

Maxwell didn't have too much time to ponder what had just happened because Angelica handed her the check.

"Three dollars and seventy-five cents for tea?" Maxwell said. "That's highway robbery."

"Cash or charge?" Angelica asked.

"I'm going to have to charge it," Maxwell told her.

"Then you can pay inside," Angelica said, walking off.

Maxwell entered the shop. The teenage boy with the dog was inside talking with a slightly older guy who was behind the counter. The guy behind the counter had tattoos and several body piercings, which seemed out of place in a quaint café like The Wooden Shoe. The bell on the door rattled when Maxwell came inside, and they both stopped talking to look at her.

"I just want to pay this," Maxwell said, handing the tattooed guy her check and her mom's credit card. *Excuse me for living,* she felt like saying because they had both given her such dirty looks.

"Our credit card terminal is in the back," the guy with the tattoos said and went to the back of the shop.

While he was gone, Maxwell took a moment to study the boy with the dog. He was average height and thin. He was wearing a baseball cap that was pulled down over his eyes, so Maxwell could barely make out his face. Come to think of it, Maxwell had never really gotten a good look at his face because he was always wearing that cap. If it hadn't been for the dog, she wouldn't even be certain he was the same boy she had seen in her neighborhood.

Moments later the tattooed guy returned with two receipts. He handed one to Maxwell. "Okay. Thanks," he said in a tone that indicated that he was anxious to be rid of her.

"Don't I have to sign something?" Maxwell asked.

"No signature required if it's under ten dollars," the tattooed guy told Maxwell.

"Okay," Maxwell said. She started toward the door. The sky was gray and it looked like it might start raining any moment. It was just her good fortune to get caught in a downpour.

"How'd we do?" she heard Angelica call from the back of the store.

One of the guys cleared his throat as Angelica came out.

"Oh, Maxwell, I thought you'd left," Angelica said, putting on her jacket. "Hey, do you want a ride home? It looks like rain."

"I'd love one," Maxwell said.

"Well, then, let's go. See you guys."

Maxwell followed Angelica outside. As they walked to Angelica's car, the first few drops of rain started to fall.

Maxwell noticed a Mobile Geeks car parked in the lot, not far from Angelica's car. She remembered seeing it in front of Mr. Bentley's house.

"Whose car is that?" she asked, trying to dodge the rain drops.

"Oh, that. It belongs to my co-worker. He's a techie. That's his other part time job."

"The guy with all the tattoos?" Maxwell asked.

"That's the one," Angelica said, unlocking the car.

"Do both of those guys work there?" Maxwell asked, climbing in.

"No," Angelica said, "Why?" She started the car.

"Oh, just curious. I got the feeling that something weird was going on, but I can't put my finger on it."

"No. The guy behind the counter works there, obviously. The other one is just a friend. He likes to hang out sometimes."

"So, you've known him a long time?" Maxwell asked.

"You could say that. Why?"

"I don't know. It just seemed to me like you didn't know him before today."

"What makes you say that?" Angelica asked.

"Well, you didn't greet him, for one, when you took his order."

"I suppose you know everything about the dos and don'ts of waiting tables," Angelica said. She looked upset.

"I'm not saying that. Never mind. Let's drop it."

"Whatever," Angelia said.

Maxwell was very quiet. She was thinking. The rain was coming down hard now. "How long have you worked at The Wooden Shoe?" she finally asked.

Angelica sighed impatiently. "Look, Maxwell, I know you like to think of yourself as an amateur sleuth and Dexter thinks it's cute and all, but the way I see it, you ask too many questions."

"Okay," Maxwell said. "I was just trying to be interested in you. You're my brother's girlfriend after all. Maybe one day you'll be family."

Angelica pulled up in front of Maxwell's house. She smiled at Maxwell, but Maxwell got the feeling it was forced.

"Just remember, curiosity is one thing. But, you know, it killed the cat."

Maxwell laughed. "Thank you for the ride and the reminder."

"I'm just saying all of your questions could get you in a lot of trouble, if you're not careful. And we both know Dexter wouldn't want that."

"Okay," Maxwell said. "Got it."

Angelica drove off, leaving Maxwell standing on the sidewalk in the rain.

"I believe that was a not-so veiled threat," she said.

There were so many questions and Maxwell was dying to investigate, but the rain was coming down in sheets, so she decided staying indoors was her best bet for the time being.

19. Friends Again

The next week passed by uneventfully. Maxwell didn't see the boy with the dog, Mr. Bentley, or Mrs. Cook once. She didn't see all that much of Kenneth either, for that matter. He stayed on his side of the planet with Britney, Darla and the other supermodels, and Maxwell stayed on her side, mostly on her own.

On Friday, Maxwell ventured into the lunch room once more and was eating her almond butter and honey sandwich at a quiet table near the window when Maria Ramsdell approached.

"Is anyone sitting here?" she asked.

"Yes," Maxwell said, smiling mischievously. "There are three of us here. Me, myself, and I."

Maria smiled. "I have the same three with me. Do you mind if we join you guys?"

"Suit yourselves," Maxwell said.

Maria sat down across from her. She had a light blue plastic tray with the day's lunch: a pulled pork sandwich, sweet potato fries, applesauce, and a carton of chocolate milk. The pulled pork looked stringy and watery, the fries seemed soggy, and the applesauce was a strange color. Maria frowned. "It always sounds better than it actually looks," she said.

"Or tastes," Maxwell said. "That's why I usually go home for lunch," Maxwell told her.

"Do you think Mrs. McQueen is going to like our project?" Maria asked.

"I hope so," Maxwell said, starting on her apple.

"Me, too. It was a good project. I thought so, anyway," Maria said.

Maxwell nodded. "I guess we'll find out soon," she said.

Neither girl said anything for a while. "Anyway," Maria finally said, "I heard about what you said to Tammi the other day."

"What do you mean 'heard about' it?" Maxwell asked.

"Everyone's talking about it. It was pretty funny. And really brave."

"Brave?" Maxwell repeated.

"No one stands up to Tammi. She says whatever she wants and we just have to take it."

"Well," Maxwell said, "I wasn't trying to be brave or funny. I was just annoyed."

Maria nodded and tried the pulled pork sandwich. She made a face.

Maxwell laughed. "I didn't know you had second lunch," she said. "I thought everyone in our class had first lunch."

"I used to," Maria said. "But I just changed my schedule last week."

"Oh," Maxwell said. "I usually go home for lunch, but maybe I'll start eating at school."

"That sounds good," Maria said. "We can eat together, if you want. I like this table. Maybe it can be our table."

Maxwell nodded. Maria wasn't so bad once you got to know her.

Later that evening, Maxwell was home alone. Her mom had gone to Orange County to see a client and was stuck in a monster traffic jam.

She had called Maxwell around 4:00 to give her the heads up. "Why don't you make yourself a chicken sandwich?" she suggested. "There are some chicken breasts in the freezer."

"Good idea," Maxwell said, rolling her eyes. The truth was she wasn't hungry. She was restless.

She hated when a case went stale. If she didn't pick up the scent soon, she was afraid all of her leads would run cold. She felt like calling Kenneth to ask him to help her brainstorm, but since they were no longer best friends, it was out of the question.

Maxwell hung up the phone and stared at the kitchen wall, as if she expected some mysterious writing to appear on it, telling her what to do.

She put her hands over her eyes. She sighed. She listened carefully. Was that barking she heard outside? No. The neighborhood was painfully quiet.

Maxwell went outside and sat on the bench in front of her house.

Nothing. Zero. Zip. Nada.

Seconds passed.

Maxwell changed her position.

"Kenneth!" she heard Mrs. Newman call from inside the Newmans' house. "Tell Amy Lynn to come downstairs."

Maxwell heard a door slam. She wanted to go next door to find out what the Newmans were up to, but she couldn't think of a good excuse.

Finally, after what seemed like hours, Maxwell heard the phone ringing inside her house. She went inside to answer it.

"May I speak to Mrs. Joelle Parker," the voice on the other end asked.

"She isn't available," Maxwell answered. "May I take a message?"

"Yes, this is the fraud protection service for her Visa account ending in zero-three-three-three. We're just checking on a charge she made last Thursday at Sports Palace for three hundred seventy-five dollars."

"Oh," Maxwell said.

"Have her call us on the toll-free number listed on the back of her card. Thank you."

"You're welcome," Maxwell said, but the caller had already hung up. She hated it when people said "thank you" to dismiss you rather than to actually thank you. It was so insincere.

Maxwell started to write a message for her mother to call the credit card company. Her mother wouldn't have spent over three hundred dollars at some place called Sports Palace, though, so it was an odd message. Maxwell put her pen down and went up to her room.

She took her emergency credit card out of the side pocket in her knapsack and carefully examined it. The last four digits were zero-three-three-three. She had used the card last Thursday at The Wooden Shoe. Maybe this was all some computer glitch.

Maxwell went to the computer and logged on to the Visa account.

She clicked on "recent transactions."

Sure enough, there was a charge for three hundred seventy-five dollars at Sports Palace in Woodland Hills on Thursday, but there was no charge for three dollars and seventy-five cents at The Wooden Shoe.

Maxwell thought fast. First of all, her mother was probably going to ground her for using the credit card to buy a cup of tea. Second, she was going kill her for this mix-up, unless she could straighten it out first. After all, the guy at The Wooden Shoe had probably just made some mistake when he ran the card.

Maxwell grabbed her knapsack and ran downstairs. She got her bike out of the garage and took off down the street towards downtown Riverdale.

The guy with the tattoos was standing behind the counter listening to an MP3 player while Angelica re-stocked the counter with jars of lingonberry jam.

"Wow, Maxwell, twice in one month," Angelica said. "What can I get you today?"

"I think I probably should talk to him," Maxwell said, pointing at the guy with the tattoos.

"About?"

"It's about my bill from last time," Maxwell said.

"Al," Angelica said loudly. "This girl wants to talk to you."

Al, formerly known as the tattooed guy, took the ear buds out of his ear. "What?" he asked.

Maxwell shook her head. Their customer service was unbelievable. "Uh. Hello, Al," she began. "I was here last week."

"Okay," he said, impatiently.

"And I bought some tea."

"Yeah," Al said.

"And I paid with a credit card."

"I don't remember that, but okay," he said with exaggerated patience.

Maxwell looked at him. "I have the receipt, but my card was never charged. Instead, some store I've never heard of charged me for a hundred times the price of the tea." She pulled a crumpled receipt from her knapsack and handed it to him.

"This is our receipt. Three seventy-five for tea. I don't know anything about the other charge." He handed the receipt back to her.

"Maybe not. But it doesn't explain why my card wasn't charged. You took it to the back and ran it. Why isn't that charge showing up online?"

"I have no idea," Al said. "That *is* weird."

"I don't understand," Maxwell said. "Maybe it's because you didn't have me sign the receipt."

"No," Al said. "That wouldn't be the problem."

"Then, what is?"

"I don't think we have a problem."

"Aren't you even concerned that I wasn't charged for the tea?"

"Look," Al said. "I don't even remember the tea or running your card. As far as I'm concerned, we're good. Thanks for coming in, but what do you want me to do?"

"Nothing. I just thought you could help, but never mind."

"That's what I'm talking about," Al said. "Now if you'll excuse me, I don't want to burn the sticky buns."

Al put his ear buds in and went to the kitchen. Maxwell glanced at Angelica, who was busy polishing the glass countertop.

"Hey," Angelica said, "look on the bright side. At least you didn't have to pay almost four bucks for a cup of tea."

Go ahead and play dumb, Maxwell thought, *but something doesn't smell right.*

Rather than push the point, however, Maxwell decided to leave.

On her way home, Maxwell passed the Riverdale Cemetery, where her father was buried. To her surprise, she saw Mrs. Cook's car parked near the entrance, and on closer inspection, she saw Mrs. Cook walking towards the grassy area, carrying a bouquet of flowers.

Maxwell found a spot nearby where she could observe Mrs. Cook without being seen.

She crouched behind a jacaranda tree and watched her elderly neighbor kneel down in front of one of the graves and start clearing away dead flowers and weeds from the site.

She worked painstakingly for several minutes. When she was finished, she walked back to her car.

Maxwell heard a car start, and seconds later, Mrs. Cook drove off.

Maxwell was itching to know which grave Mrs. Cook had been visiting, but first, she stopped at her father's grave, which was just a few rows away. She sat down and looked at her surroundings. Night was falling. She hoped her mother would be home by now.

"Mom will be wondering where I am," Maxwell said aloud, trying to convince herself she was not alone in a cemetery at nightfall. "So, I guess I'd better go on home. I can always come back. That grave's not going anywhere. I can come back tomorrow to find out who's buried there." She stood up and started to walk her bike to the pavement, when suddenly she heard a loud "Boo!"

Maxwell stopped in her tracks and caught her breath as someone lunged at her from behind a large, ornate headstone.

"You jerk!" she cried when she saw that it was Kenneth, but she was too relieved to be angry with him.

"I scared you, didn't I?" Kenneth said, doubling over with laughter.

"You did not."

"You should have seen how high you jumped. You thought I was some creepy ghost."

"Correction. I thought you were a creepy weirdo who likes snooping around graveyards at night. Kenny, what are you doing here so late?"

"Following Mrs. Cook."

"What?"

"Yeah, I told you I noticed she goes somewhere every Friday evening, so today, I decided to follow her."

"Wow," Maxwell said, "I'm impressed."

"What about you, Max?"

"It's a long story. But I just happened to see Mrs. Cook as I was riding by. She was leaving flowers at a grave."

"Whose grave?"

"I don't know. I was going to wait until tomorrow, but now that you're here, let's find out."

Maxwell led Kenneth to the grave she had seen Mrs. Cook kneeling in front of.

"Levi Cook," Maxwell read. She sighed. "He died five years ago, not this summer."

"It could be a relative—her husband's brother or father."

"No, it's her husband. She didn't kill him."

"Cheer up, Max, maybe she killed someone else. I mean, why else would she be digging a grave in her backyard?"

Maxwell smiled at Kenneth. "You're absolutely right. Someone's buried back there and we owe it to, well, you know, society, to find out who it is."

"Exactly." Kenneth looked so accommodating and friendly that Maxwell had to fight the enormous impulse she felt to hug him right there on the spot.

"Look, Kenny, about that day—I'm sorry I was so..."

"Rude."

"Well, yes, and for..."

"Yelling at me and telling me to go away." Kenneth was smiling. "Forget about it. I have."

"Obviously."

"You're lucky. I never take anything you say seriously, Max."

"In that case, I suppose you don't care to know that I told Veronica off. You were right—about my selling my soul. I guess I really thought she'd be my friend if I kept helping her. But she wasn't and she never would have been." Maxwell looked at Kenneth. "I think I knew that all along. I was just pretending that she liked me. I guess I have a pretty active imagination."

Kenneth looked around. The sun was just about gone. "Let's get out of here, Maxwell. Please."

Maxwell and Kenneth didn't say much as they rode together, but when they got home, Kenneth asked, "Are we still going to investigate Mrs. Cook?"

"I don't know. It's weird, but I don't think I ever really believed she was a murderer. I just made all of that stuff up. I guess you could say I exaggerated the facts."

"But what about the digging? I heard that with my own ears."

Maxwell explained how she had seen a cat digging in Mrs. Cook's backyard one night. "I'll bet that was the noise we heard that night."

"And what about the man I saw?"

"Probably a friend or, more likely, a mover. I guess I knew that all along, too. I only pretended that I believed she was a murderer."

"In that case, Max, I have something to show you." Kenneth riffled through his pockets and finally pulled out a crumpled printout from the Internet. "I Googled her," he said, handing it to Maxwell.

"'E.B. Cunningham is an American crime writer of both mainstream and young adult fiction. Most of her novels feature female detectives who are proficient at solving mysteries. E.B. Cunningham is the *nom de plume* for Mrs. Edna Cook of Riverdale, California.'" Maxwell stopped reading. "How, in heaven's name did I miss this? My mom even has one of her books!" Maxwell covered her face with her hands. "I should have known, Kenny. You're going to think twice before listening to another one of my crazy ideas."

"It's okay, Max. You may not be like most girls, but that's why I like you."

Maxwell smiled. She remembered her dream about Harry Connick, Jr. and how he said he couldn't love her because he didn't know the real her.

"Are you sure you wouldn't rather hang out with Britney?" Maxwell asked. "She seems to like you."

"No, she giggles too much. Besides, she's always touching my hair. It gets on my nerves."

"See you tomorrow, Kenneth."

The lights were on, so Maxwell knew her mother had made it home.

Maxwell left her bike outside and went inside her house. She went straight to her room, opened her knapsack, and took out her notebook. Turning to the first blank page, she wrote the following:

1. Mrs. Cook is a widow, NOT a murderer.
2. The boy with the dog and Mr. Bentley know each other, which is weird, to say the least.
3. The boy with the dog has been seen tampering with other people's garbage bins.
4. There is a credit card ring active at large that is known for rummaging through people's garbage bins (Coincidence? I think not!).
5. I used my credit card in a place where the boy with the dog and a weird tattooed guy named Al were seen engrossed in a conversation, and now I

have a fraudulent charge on my card.

6. Al is denying any involvement with my credit card.

7. I think the boy with the dog is somehow involved in the credit card ring.

8. Mr. Bentley is probably involved, too. Al may be their stooge.

9. I have no idea what Angelica's deal is, but she is acting VERY STRANGE! Should I tell Dexter or let him find out on his own????

Maxwell thought long and hard, trying to determine if there were any other strange facts she should list.

She remembered the night she'd left her mom's camera rolling. Maybe she had inadvertently gotten some incriminating footage.

Maxwell got the camera and brought it to her room. She turned it on, located the movie, and hit "play."

At first it looked like a still photo of the neighborhood. Nothing happened for ten full minutes. Maxwell hit the fast-forward button.

Suddenly, something on the screen caught her eye. Could that be what she thought it was? She hit the rewind button. "Hmm," she said as she watched it again.

She went to her mother's room and plugged the camera into her mother's laptop.

When the video had uploaded, Maxwell watched it again on the bigger screen.

"Okay," she said, "At least, now I know." She was very calm on the outside, but inside she felt excited.

She walked over to the window and looked out. The white carpet cleaning van was gone. The neighborhood was quiet.

Maxwell wondered if she had misunderstood the clues. After all, she had been wrong about Mrs. Cook.

Maxwell sighed. She put on her pajamas and went to bed.

Maybe things would look up in the morning.

20. Kidnapped!

The next day, Saturday, was a long day. The morning dragged. Maxwell spent most of it doing science homework. After lunch, her mother made her go with her on errands. First they went grocery shopping. Then they dropped off her mother's dry cleaning. Next it was off to the bank. Maxwell didn't think they would ever finish.

"Let's get a frozen yogurt," her mother said, just when Maxwell thought they could head home.

"Okay," Maxwell said, reluctantly, but she had to admit, the red velvet and cake batter swirl hit the spot.

She was still finishing her yogurt when they pulled into their driveway. She helped her mom bring the bags inside and was getting ready to help put the groceries away when her mom said, "Don't worry, Maxwell. I'll put everything up. I'm sure you have something else you'd rather be doing. You've sacrificed enough of your Saturday on the altar of mundane chores."

"Thanks, Mom," Maxwell said. "I'll see you later."

By now, it was mid-afternoon. Maxwell went up to her room and looked down on Mulberry Avenue. The white van was back, parked down the street.

Good, Maxwell thought. *Time to investigate.* She put on her vest and deducing hat, grabbed her binoculars, and went downstairs.

She slowly opened the front door and stepped outside, stealthily making her way to the bench, where she surreptitiously sat, crouched behind the rubber tree. She held the binoculars up to her eyes and watched the van.

Maxwell maintained her position for several moments.

After a while, the neighborhood dogs started barking, and sure enough, the boy with the dog appeared. As he approached the van he crossed the street and walked several feet ahead of it. Then he turned and, ever so slightly, looked at the van. He made a gesture with his hand and then walked away.

Maxwell was dying to know what it all meant. Before she knew what she was doing, and against her better judgment, she stood up and began walking directly toward the van.

The front seats were empty and the back of the van was blocked off by a metal screen. Maxwell walked around to the back of the van. The back windows were covered with a film, so she couldn't see into the back from that angle either.

She listened carefully and thought she heard a faint electronic humming sound coming from inside the van. She was about to get a little closer to investigate, when the side door of the van opened.

All of a sudden, a man emerged from the van, grabbed her, pulled her inside, and closed the door.

Maxwell immediately went into survival mode. She tried screaming, but her assailant's strong hand was covering her mouth, stifling her cries. She tried scratching but only managed to flail her arms helplessly as her kidnapper deftly stayed out of harm's way.

"You're perfectly safe," he kept saying. "No one here wants to hurt you."

As if she could trust that. Someone who grabs you and pulls you into a cargo van is not the type of person who should be taken at his word. Maxwell tried to scream again. She wished her mother could hear her.

"Promise me you'll stop screaming if I move my hand," the kidnapper said.

"Never!" Maxwell tried to say. Eventually, she had to stop fighting, but she didn't want her kidnappers to get the idea that she had given up, so even though she couldn't use her physical strength to fight, she decided to use her brain. She studied her surroundings carefully.

The van's interior was rather dark, but her eyes soon adjusted to the low light. There appeared to be a great deal of electronic equipment—monitors and recording devices—and at least, two people, in addition to the man who was holding her: another man and a woman. All three were dressed in dark clothes and wore dark baseball caps.

They were all watching her intently. None of them made any threatening moves in her direction, which Maxwell interpreted as a good sign or, at least, an opportunity.

Finally, one of the men pulled out a black leather wallet. "We're the FBI," he said, showing her his badge. It had his name, Special Agent Jordan Howard, and a small photograph.

"So, you'll stop screaming?" the other one asked. "I'm moving my hand," he said. He placed her down and carefully backed away from her. "Now you sit still while we explain what's going on."

"First of all, what did you think you were doing?" the woman asked.

Maxwell folded her arms and stared back. "You're all FBI?" she asked.

"Special Agents Browning, Howard and Lowe."

"Sounds like a law firm," Maxwell mumbled.

The female agent, Special Agent Lowe, looked like she was trying not to laugh. "So, tell us, what were you doing out there? And don't say you were looking for your cat or try to make up some story. We've been watching you, Maxwell."

"How did you know my name?" Maxwell asked.

"We're the FBI. We know everything. What were you doing?"

Maxwell sighed. "I was investigating."

"What were you investigating?" asked Special Agent Howard. He was tall, dark, and distractingly good-looking.

"Different things," Maxwell said, trying not to stare at him. "That kid with the dog, for one."

"What else?" Special Agent Howard asked.

"My neighbor."

"Yes. About your neighbor. What do you know about him?" This time Special Agent Browning asked the question. Special Agent Browning had curly red hair and a comical expression.

"His name is Mr. Bentley. He works from home. He's a computer programmer. I don't know much more than that, except I know when he's home and when he goes out. Things like that," Maxwell told them.

"You know what he wants you to know," said Special Agent Howard.

"What does that mean?" Maxwell asked.

"Your Mr. Bentley is a pretty creative guy. His name is really Reginald Penbrooke-Jones. He's a British national and an International thief wanted by Scotland Yard and Interpol. We've had him under surveillance for months. You almost compromised our stakeout," Special Agent Browning told her.

"How?" Maxwell asked. "What did I do?"

"That guy you were following is one of ours," Special Agent Browning said.

"The boy with the dog is an agent?" Maxwell asked.

"Yes, his name is Mitchell. The dog's Harvey," Special Agent Lowe told her.

"But he looks like a regular kid," Maxwell said.

"He's one of our best undercover agents for that reason. Penbrooke-Jones has been recruiting young boys to help run his credit card/identity theft ring. We had Mitchell pose as a world-class hacker to get Penbrooke-Jones' attention. He's been Penbrooke-Jones' number one man for several months now. They have a bunch of kids working at local businesses," Special Agent Howard added.

"Like The Wooden Shoe! I knew it!" Maxwell exclaimed.

"Yes. They mine for information, skim credit cards. It's a very complicated operation," Special Agent Howard continued.

"So, when Mitchell drops stuff in Mr. Bentley's—I mean Mr. Penbrooke-Jones' garbage bin—?"

"Mitchell hides data in those bags that look like doggie bags. Then he makes the drop. Penbrooke-Jones uses the data to steal identities and with that, millions of dollars," said Lowe.

"Wow. Who knew?" Maxwell asked, incredulously.

"You did, sort of," Special Agent Lowe said, smiling at Maxwell.

"What should we do with her?" Special Agent Browning asked, frowning.

"I don't know. It's pretty serious. There are laws governing this sort of thing," Special Agent Lowe said.

"But I didn't break any laws," Maxwell protested. "I'm not a criminal. In fact, I'm one of the victims. There's a fraudulent charge on my credit card."

"Should we call the chief?" Special Agent Browning asked, ignoring Maxwell's protests.

"He won't be happy," Special Agent Howard said.

"I promise I won't do it again," Maxwell said. "And whatever you do, please, please, please don't tell my mom. She'll have my head."

"We're kidding. But we do have a favor to ask," Special Agent Lowe said, smiling again.

"So, remember, all we want you to do is keep him distracted for about ten minutes while we search his house. That's all we need. We don't need you to try to get him to admit anything. You'll be wearing a wire and an earpiece, but that's just so we can monitor the situation and make sure you're not in any danger, and in case we need to communicate with you. Just act natural and make him think he's looking for a baseball," Special Agent Howard was saying.

"But, he probably knows I don't play with baseballs. He's going to know the whole thing's a setup," Maxwell said.

All three agents were standing in front of Maxwell scrutinizing her.

"Do you think he'll suspect anything?" Special Agent Howard asked them.

"Nah," Special Agent Browning said, "she looks so innocent, it's a crime."

Thank goodness there's no pressure, Maxwell thought to herself. She hoped the sarcasm would soothe her nerves. Her heart was pounding away. She felt like she was going to pass out.

21. Mr. Bentley and the Baseball

Maxwell marched up to Mr. Bentley's front door and rang the doorbell.

After several moments, he answered the door. "What can I do for you, Maxwell? Selling Girl Scout cookies?"

"No. I'm sorry to bother you, but Kenneth and I were playing ball, and I accidentally threw the ball into your yard. Can you please get it for me?" Maxwell asked, talking fast.

"Where did you say you threw it?"

"Well, I was trying to throw it to Kenneth, but it landed in your backyard. I can show you exactly where it landed."

"Now?"

"Yes. We're in the middle of a game."

Mr. Bentley/Penbrooke-Jones hesitated. He seemed annoyed. But he opened the door a bit wider and said, "Come on, let's go. Where's this ball?" He led Maxwell through the house to the backyard.

Mr. Bentley's house was very sparsely decorated, all steely gray and white. The furniture was square with sharp angles and corners. There were no pillows, no photographs. Everything was sterile and impersonal. Maxwell shivered.

"It's in the ice plants covering the hilly part of your yard, near the fence," Maxwell said.

Mr. Bentley walked toward the back fence. "Over here?" he asked.

"No, somewhere over here," Maxwell said, waving her hand in a circular motion. She started looking in the plants a few feet away from where he was standing. Mr. Bentley joined her and they searched the ground covering for several minutes.

"Are you sure it landed in my yard?" he asked.

"It was right here," Maxwell said, emphatically, pointing at the ground. "I'm positive. Maybe it rolled away. This hill is pretty steep."

Now Mr. Bentley looked really impatient. "Can't you just get another ball?" he asked through his gritted teeth.

"No, Mr. Bentley, I have to find it. It's my brother's baseball. Hank Aaron autographed it. My brother will kill me if I've lost it. Please. I've got to find it."

"Why were you playing with the ball if it was so valuable?"

"I couldn't find another one, and I wanted to practice for P.E. I'm not really good in P.E. My teacher, Mrs. Robins has it in for me. I wanted to try to get better, so my friend Kenneth was helping me. Baseball's not really his sport. He's more into basketball, not that he's not good at baseball. He's good at all sports. Well, maybe not curling, but most of the mainstream sports. The ones we usually play in junior high school. Like dodge ball. Did you ever play dodge ball, Mr. Bentley?" Mr. Bentley was intently looking for the baseball, but Maxwell could tell her chatter was distracting him. She hoped the FBI was making quick work of their search.

"A few more minutes, Maxwell, we're almost done," Special Agent Browning said in her ear, as if on cue.

"I must confess," Mr. Bentley began.

Oh, no, Maxwell thought. *He's going to confess to the identify thefts. Then he's going to have to kill me and bury me beneath the ice plants.* Now they'd have to call her biopic *...and She Was Never Heard From Again....*

Maxwell started to back away.

"Where do you think you're going?" Mr. Bentley asked, grabbing her arm. "If I have to search, so do you."

"I thought I saw something white under that bush." Maxwell said. "But it was a mushroom."

"As I was saying," Mr. Bentley began again. "I must confess—"

"You know, you really don't have to confess anything to me," Maxwell said. "I mean, after all, I'm just a kid. Nobody's going to even listen to me, anyway—"

"—that I was a pretty good athlete when I was your age," Mr. Bentley continued.

"Oh," Maxwell said. "Well, good for you. That's great. That's excellent!"

"Calm down, Max, you're doing great," Special Agent Browning said in her ear.

Maxwell felt like she was going to hyperventilate. She was a horrible liar. Mr. Bentley was going to see right through her charade. After all, he was a hardened criminal, probably one of the best liars in the world.

Finally, Special Agent Browning said, "We got it, Maxwell. Get out of there."

When she was sure Mr. Bentley wasn't looking she pulled a baseball out of her knapsack and placed it on the ground amid the ice plants. "Hey! Would you look at that! It's right here," she said, picking it up and showing it to Mr. Bentley.

Mr. Bentley looked disgusted. "Brilliant," he said. "Why don't you let yourself out the side gate?"

"Thanks a million," Maxwell yelled, as she quickly walked to the gate. "You literally saved my life."

"Now go home, Maxwell," Special Agent Browning said. "This could get dangerous. It's no place for an amateur detective."

Maxwell's breathing returned to somewhat normal. She hurried home, without giving Mr. Bentley's (aka Mr. Penbrooke-Jones') house a second look.

22. The Bust

The next morning Maxwell got up early and went into her mother's room.

Mrs. Parker was sitting up in bed, sketching.

"Can I see?" Maxwell asked.

Mrs. Parker pulled the covers down. "Hop in," she said.

Maxwell hopped in, and Mrs. Parker put her arm around her. "New designs for the new line," she told her.

"Nice," Maxwell said as she snuggled her head against her mother's arm. "Anything on TV?"

"I don't know," Mrs. Parker said, "probably just the news at this hour."

"Oh, that," Maxwell said, offhandedly. She took the remote and turned the TV on.

"And now, in local news," the male anchor was saying, "a man posing as a computer programmer was apprehended yesterday with the help of an alert citizen, and is now in police custody. Here's Wink Williamson, live in Riverdale, with more."

Wink Williamson proceeded to launch into a recap of the crimes as video footage played in the background.

Maxwell watched the screen nervously. She cleared her throat several times.

After a few moments, Mrs. Parker looked up. "Maxwell," she said, "isn't that our street?"

"Yes."

"Do you know anything about this?"

"Well, sort of."

"What, exactly, does, 'well, sort of' mean?"

"I guess it kind of means that I'm the 'alert citizen.' I helped the FBI bust Mr. Bentley—who is really a Bad Guy wanted on multiple continents—yesterday."

"You did what?"

"Don't get mad. I was spying on Mrs. Cook, so I used your camera. I didn't know what I had until yesterday. I wasn't trying to bust the Backstreet Bandits. I mean, seriously, who knew?"

Mrs. Parker was staring at Maxwell.

Oh, great, here it comes, Maxwell thought.

To her surprise, Mrs. Parker smiled. "Maxwell, you amaze me," she said. "You did all this and didn't say anything. You could have been hurt."

"I literally stumbled into it, Mom. I forgot your camcorder outside one night. I was investigating Mrs. Cook, but I had no idea what was going on right under my nose. Some detective, huh? Pursuing a fake suspect, almost letting the real perpetrators get away."

"May I remind you that you're just a little girl?" Mrs. Parker said.

"I'm twelve," Maxwell said.

"Exactly. You could have been hurt," Mrs. Parker said again, hugging Maxwell. "But, just think, you helped bust…Mr. Bentley and the bandits. It's really amazing. No, that's not big enough. Maxwell, you're practically a crime-busting hero."

"Mom. It was nothing, really," Maxwell said. She was starting to feel a bit embarrassed.

"But you have to promise me you'll never do anything like this again."

"I think I'm done with detective work."

"But, you're so good at it."

"Don't make fun of me."

"I'm not, Sweetie. What I'm trying to say is, you have a unique way of seeing things. Just be careful. I don't want to lose you." She kissed Maxwell on her forehead. "What do you say to pancakes?"

"Sounds great."

Mrs. Parker climbed out of bed. As she passed the window, she stopped. "What in tarnation?" she exclaimed. Maxwell jumped out of bed and joined her at the window.

Mulberry Avenue was swarming with police and FBI agents. Yellow police tape was everywhere, roping things in, keeping things out, bobbing and weaving its way through the street like a dragon at a Chinese New Year parade. The police were examining the street, the garbage bins, and walking up and down people's yards. There were official-looking people standing in front of black SUVs, talking on radios.

Special Agents Browning, Howard and Lowe were standing on the sidewalk in front of Mr. Bentley's house. Special Agent Lowe noticed Maxwell at the window and nodded to her. She nudged Special Agent Browning, who in turn nudged Special Agent Howard. They all waved discreetly at Maxwell.

Maxwell waved and smiled back. Thanks to them, her mother would never know about the fraudulent charge on her credit card. Someone at the Bureau had been able to make it go away.

The pancakes were delicious, but every time Maxwell looked up, she found her mother staring at her. Twice, she reached across the table and patted Maxwell's hand.

"Mom," Maxwell finally said, "I'm not going anywhere."

"I know," Mrs. Parker said.

Maxwell started to take the dirty dishes to the sink.

"Leave them, Honey. I'll do the dishes. You go...do something fun."

Maxwell slowly left the kitchen, glancing back at her mom several times. *Who is this woman, and what has she done with Mom?* she wondered.

She went into the family room and started to play the piano.

After a while, she heard the doorbell and a few moments later, her mother called, "Maxwell! Can you come here for a minute?"

Maxwell closed the piano and joined her mother at the front door.

Two men in dark suits were talking to Mrs. Parker.

"Maxwell, this is Lieutenant Williams and Lieutenant Bobson. Gentlemen, my daughter, Maxwell."

The two men shook Maxwell's hand.

"Special Agents Browning, Howard and Lowe told us you're the little girl responsible for all of this," Lieutenant Bobson said, gesturing at the police activity outside.

Maxwell took exception to the 'little girl' reference, but noting their guns, decided not to comment on it. She always knew her dimples would be a liability.

"Thank you for your detective work, young lady. Thanks to you, people's identities will be safe again, at least in this community," Lieutenant Williams said.

"It was no big deal," Maxwell said modestly.

"It was a very big deal, young lady. Good detective work. You helped the investigation move forward. So, from two detectives to another, thanks again."

The two detectives walked back to their car.

Mrs. Parker shut the door. She couldn't seem to stop smiling. "Well?" she asked, expectantly.

"What, Mom?"

"You're not as excited as I thought you'd be."

"Didn't they seem a bit, I don't know...regular? They weren't wearing hats or trench coats, there was no cool private eye lingo, and to be honest, Lieutenant Bobson looked eerily like my math teacher."

"What did you expect, Maxwell? Humphrey Bogart?"

"Yeah. Kind of."

Mrs. Parker laughed. She was about to go into the kitchen when the doorbell rang again.

This time it was Mrs. Cook.

"Hello, Mrs. Parker," she said. "I was finally able to get out of my house, and I wanted to come over and see the girl of the hour."

"She's right here," Mrs. Parker said.

"Hi, Mrs. Cook," Maxwell said.

"Hello, Maxwell. Good work. The detectives told me how you helped them solve the case."

"It was nothing."

"Would you like to sit down, Mrs. Cook," Mrs. Parker asked.

"Well, sure. I have a few minutes. And I must confess, I've wanted a chance to talk to the woman responsible for this lovely little person."

"I don't know that I'm responsible for Maxwell. She's pretty much her own person," Mrs. Parker said, smiling at Maxwell. "But, I am immensely proud of her. I just hope she hasn't been too much of a bother to you."

"Not at all," Mrs. Cook said, following Mrs. Parker into the living room. "I only wish she'd visit me more often."

"Can I get you some tea?" Maxwell asked.

"I would love a cup of tea," Mrs. Cook said.

"And you, Mom?"

"Sure."

"What a sweetheart," Maxwell heard Mrs. Cook say as she went into the kitchen.

"She's like my right hand," Mrs. Parker said. "I'd be lost without her."

"Well," said Maxwell as she filled the teakettle with water. "Who knew?" She put the kettle on the stove and waited for the water to boil.

A few minutes later, Maxwell took a tray of tea and cookies into the living room.

By now, Mrs. Cook and her mom were chatting like old friends.

"I know," Mrs. Cook was saying, "I know. It's not easy losing a husband. And you were so young."

Mrs. Parker looked up at Maxwell. "It turns out Mrs. Cook, I mean Edna, and I have a lot in common."

"I knew you would," Maxwell said, setting a cup of tea in front of each of them. "If you need anything else, I'll be upstairs."

"See what I mean?" Mrs. Parker asked, and the two women laughed softly.

Maxwell went up to her room and sat down at her desk.

"What a day," she said, "and it's not even noon."

Maxwell went to the window and looked out.

The last police car was just leaving Mulberry Avenue. Everything seemed back to normal.

From the Newmans' house, Maxwell could hear Sabrina fighting with Mrs. Newman.

"You're so five years ago!" Sabrina yelled.

"You're not getting a tattoo, and that's the last I want to hear about it, young lady!" Mrs. Newman yelled back.

Maxwell sat down at her desk and took her notebook out and wrote:

Case No. 0362—The Cook Murders...SOLVED.

Then on the next line, she wrote:

Case No. 0363—Is Angelica mixed up with the Backstreet Bandits???

She turned the page.

<u>Plan of Action</u>

1. Return to The Wooden Shoe (with Kenneth) to investigate.

2. <u>Do not</u> tell Dexter until you are <u>absolutely certain</u> of Angelica's involvement or, at least, until you have irrefutable proof.

3. Find a vest that looks more like the ones the FBI agents wear.

23. Fishponds and Mermaids

The first thing Maxwell did when she woke up on Sunday morning was call Dexter.

"Who is this?" Dexter sounded groggy.

"It's Maxwell."

"Oh, hello." There was a long pause. "Who am I?"

Maxwell laughed. Dexter was definitely not a morning person. "Dexter, I'm sending you a nice hot cup of freshly brewed cyber coffee through the phone. Did you get it?"

"I got it—it tastes delicious, almost like the real thing. There's nothing like the artificial high you get from cyber coffee," Dexter answered. "What's up, my pet?"

"Nothing really."

Dexter groaned. "You called me at six o'clock on a Sunday morning for 'nothing really'? Spot, everyone knows, 'nothing really' can wait until after lunch. And everyone knows it's a lie, even then."

Maxwell laughed. "Sorry, Sleeping Beauty. Pardon the interruption."

"Absolutely no problem, my pet. Anyway, I have knowledge that this is far from a 'nothing really' phone call. I have information that a ticker-tape parade is in order."

"Mom told you about the Backstreet Bandits?"

"The whole shebang. Way to go, Spot!"

"It was nothing."

"It certainly was not nothing. And I apologize for that weird double-negative, but seeing as how I'm still asleep…we'll definitely talk more about this later on, Little Missy."

"Dexter, before you go, I just wanted to talk to you to let you know that I almost had an emotional crisis, but I'm fine now. I decided that you were right. The best thing is to be, you know, true to who you are. I think I finally have the courage to be myself. It's really hard to be twelve-and-a-half, you know."

"I know. I remember twelve-and-a-half. I hate to be the bearer of horrible news, Spot, but it only gets worse from there on. I'm starting to suspect things get easier when you turn, I don't know, maybe fifty."

"Why'd you have to tell me that?"

"Because I think you're old enough to handle the truth. So, what helped you get through your crisis?"

"The things you said, mostly, but Kenneth helped, too."

"That basketball playing squirt is good for something?"

"Dexter, be nice. You both helped, but I figured a few things out for myself."

"Well, I'm glad. I was a little worried about you for a while. You seemed so down this summer, and Mom told me how you'd been moping around the house."

"She noticed?"

"Of course, and she was worried, but we knew you'd be all right. You're a pretty tough cookie, Spot."

"I am, aren't I? I was surprised to find that out. But do you know what I found out about selling out? The price is too high. We're worth a lot more than some so-called friendship."

"Beautifully put, Spot. I wish I could talk more, but Archie's bugging me to use the phone. He claims it's an emergency, but I think he just wants to order a pizza."

"That *is* an emergency."

"Yeah, it is for Archie. Thanks for calling me. I love you to pieces."

"I love you to pieces too, Dexter."

"Say 'hi' to Mom for me."

Maxwell hung up and looked out of her window. Mrs. Cook was outside, taking her garbage out.

Maybe she's disposing of her latest victim, Maxwell thought, from sheer habit. A few days ago she would have felt the urge to run downstairs with a pair of gloves and a camera; today all she felt was an overwhelming desire to take out her own garbage.

Maxwell stepped out into the cool, damp, morning air, carrying a trash bag.

Mrs. Cook spotted Maxwell and waved. "Hello, Maxwell. Do you have a minute? I have something to show you."

Maxwell put the trash bag in the garbage bin. "I'll be right over," she called.

Maxwell ran to the den and grabbed a book from the bookcase. She put it in her knapsack and hurried over to Mrs. Cook's house.

Mrs. Cook led Maxwell to her backyard. "Voilà!" she said proudly. There was a fishpond where the large hole had been.

"I made it all myself," Mrs. Cook was saying. "I dug the hole, poured the cement. I even laid the stones. I'm going to the garden supply store later today to buy some aquatic plants. Would you like to come help me pick them out?"

"I'd love to go," Maxwell told her, circling the pond. "This is so cool. Look at all of that koi."

"My husband would have been so proud," Mrs. Cook said.

"I'm sure he would have, Mrs. Cook."

"That reminds me, I should pick up some rose bushes while I'm there. I like to take flowers to the cemetery on Friday evenings, and roses were his favorite."

"Mine, too, especially the little white ones."

"My husband would have loved you, Maxwell."

"Mrs. Cook, I hope you don't think it's an imposition, but would you mind signing this book?" Maxwell handed Mrs. Cook a copy of *It Never Rains in Baltimore.*

Mrs. Cook looked surprised. "How did you know E.B. Cunningham and I are one and the same?"

"I've been investigating you since you moved in," Maxwell confessed. "But my friend, Kenny, actually found out about the books. I thought you were a murderer."

"Murderess," Mrs. Cook corrected. "In my novels, I always call the female villains murderesses. It has a much more romantic ring, don't you think?" There was a twinkle in her eye. "So, you knew there was something not quite right about me, did you?"

"Well..." Maxwell began.

"Don't apologize. I consider it an honor to be 'outed' by a fellow crime-solver."

"Really?" Maxwell asked.

"Of course. I knew there was something special about you the first time I met you. Never doubt an instinct, Maxwell, that's my first motto in solving mysteries."

"Mrs. Cook," Maxwell said, "I just have one question."

"Shoot."

"Who's Marty?"

"Marty's my agent. How do you know about him?"

"It's a long story," Maxwell said.

Mrs. Cook chuckled. "I see. Well, in that case, I won't ask you to divulge any trade secrets. Now, about those plants. I'll pick you up this afternoon, okay?"

Maxwell agreed and went home.

Kenneth came outside as Maxwell was going inside.

"Hi, Max, I was just coming over to see you."

"Oh. Well, would you like to come in?"

Kenneth followed her into the house.

"Have you eaten, yet?" Maxwell asked.

"Nope."

"Well, I was getting ready to have some cereal. Do you want some?"

"Sure."

Kenneth followed Maxwell into the kitchen and sat down at the breakfast bar.

"So, what can I get for you?" Maxwell opened a cabinet and pulled out three boxes of cereal. "We have some cereal that looks like twigs and berries and some cereal that tastes like twigs and bark. Or we have some yummy granola."

"I'll have the granola."

"An excellent selection." Maxwell got two bowls and a carton of milk and placed them on the counter. She sat down next to Kenneth.

"Wait! I forgot the juice. What kind would you like, orange or carrot?" She started to get up, but Kenneth grabbed her arm.

"Wait, Maxwell, I have something for you."

"You have something? For me?"

"Yes, I got you something. It's nothing, really..."

...Maxwell and Kenneth had been married a whole year. They honeymooned in France, and now they were back to celebrate their anniversary. They were dining in a quaint little café they'd discovered on their honeymoon—modest furnishings, but great food and excellent atmosphere. There was even a little man outside selling his original paintings of the city.

Kenneth looked ravishing in his tuxedo. Maxwell was wearing a midnight-blue satin evening gown and long white gloves.

Kenneth stared deeply into her eyes as he pulled a small gold box tied with a red ribbon from his coat pocket.

"Oh, Kenneth Darling, not another diamond," she said. No, that didn't sound right.

"Oh, Kenneth, you're too good to me." No. Somehow that wasn't it either...

"I just wanted you to have it," Kenneth was saying. He handed Maxwell the box.

"What is it?" Maxwell asked. It wasn't the sophisticated response she had been looking for, but it was the best she could manage in real life.

"Open it."

Maxwell opened the box. Inside was a small glass mermaid.

"It's beautiful, Kenny."

"It wasn't very expensive—you don't have to keep it if you don't like it."

"I love it."

"I got it from the glass guy at the farmers' market. It reminded me of you, because you said you felt like a mermaid and everything. So I bought it because—I don't know—it just reminded me of you. But after what you did the other day—the way you finally stood up for yourself—I wanted you to have it—to remind you that you are a mermaid—and that I like you that way. Don't ever change."

Maxwell didn't know what to say. Kenneth shifted uncomfortably on his stool.

"Thank you, Kenneth."

"Well, we *are* buddies, right?"

Maxwell smiled. "Forever. I'm going to put this up. I'll be right back."

Maxwell ran up to her room. She wanted to find the perfect spot for Kenneth's mermaid. She looked around, and suddenly she knew exactly where it belonged.

She put the mermaid on the top shelf of her bookcase, next to the music box her father had given her when she was a little girl and the porcelain piano player from Dexter.

Maxwell closed the door to her room. She was about to go back downstairs, when she stopped and rested against the banister.

Kenneth was downstairs waiting for her to have breakfast with him, almost as if they were married, eating breakfast together before going to work...

He was a professional basketball player with the Lakers and she was a TV news anchor. They had a beach house in Malibu, an apartment in Manhattan, and tons of celebrity friends. Their celebrity couple name was Kenwell. For the third year in a row, "People" magazine dubbed them Hollywood's most adorable couple. And when Kenneth accepted his MVP he said, "I dedicate this to Max—my wife, my muse, the fulfillment of all my dreams, my MVP..."

"Maxwell, are you coming down? Your granola's getting soggy," Kenneth called.

Maxwell laughed softly. "Coming," she called, running downstairs.

"Hey, Kenny," she said as she entered the kitchen, "you'll never guess what happened yesterday."

CPSIA information can be obtained
at www.ICGtesting.com
Printed in the USA
LVOW12s2102080817

544258LV00003B/590/P